I0586260

EDITORIAL REVIEW

Thor's Dragon Rider
Book Six

Shrouded

"Thor, Kara, and some of their fellow Valkyries and friends visit the underworld in a bold effort to rescue Balder, a fallen god who has landed there by mistake. The vibrant descriptions, action-packed scenes, and some occasional well-placed humor will appeal to readers who enjoy fantasies about the legendary Valkyries." Angela M., Line Editor, Red Adept Editing

"Kara and her fellow Valkyries join Thor on a quest to retrieve Balder from Helheim in the riveting sixth installment of this Norse mythology-inspired fantasy." Alyssa B., Proofreader, Red Adept Editing

Hoodwinked

Relinquished

Shrouded

Assigned

More To Come

EDITORIAL REVIEW

Thor's Dragon Rider
Book Six

Shrouded

"Thor, Kara, and some of their fellow Valkyries and friends visit the underworld in a bold effort to rescue Balder, a fallen god who has landed there by mistake. The vibrant descriptions, action-packed scenes, and some occasional well-placed humor will appeal to readers who enjoy fantasies about the legendary Valkyries." Angela M., Line Editor, Red Adept Editing

"Kara and her fellow Valkyries join Thor on a quest to retrieve Balder from Helheim in the riveting sixth installment of this Norse mythology-inspired fantasy." Alyssa B., Proofreader, Red Adept Editing

Shrouded

Ebook first published in USA in October 2021 by Cosy Burrow Books

Ebook first published in Great Britain in October 2021 by Cosy Burrow Books

www.katrinacopebooks.com

Text Copyright © 2021 by Katrina Cope

Cover Design Copyright © art4artists.com.au

The moral right of Katrina Cope to be identified as the author of this work has been asserted

All rights reserved

No part of this publication may be reproduced or transmitted by any means, electronic, mechanical, photocopying or otherwise, without the prior permission of the publisher

This book is a work of fiction. Any references or suggestions herein to actual historical events, real people or actual locations are fictitious. All names, characterisations, locations, incidents, and fabrications are solely the product of the author's imagination, and any, and all, resemblance to actual persons alive or dead or locations or events is entirely coincidental.

Published by Cosy Burrow Books

All rights reserved

ISBN : 978-0-6450874-5-1

❀ Created with Vellum

To the readers who race to order my next book. Thank you.

A dishonorable death, hunted by criminals, and souls severed.

Asgard mourns a beloved god who should spend his afterlife in Valhalla but died out of battle, trapping him in Helheim. Following orders from Odin and his wife, Frigg, Thor takes Kara and the combined Valkyrie and dragon entourage to the underworld in hopes of attaining his release.

Impossible demands must be fulfilled, and the threats the group faces require the skills of every companion.

Will a soul be lost to save a soul?

- Chapter One -

Sleipnir's hooves clop on the hard earth moments before Elan climbs out of the hole in Yggdrasil's trunk. Eerie tendrils of mist surround us, thickening the darkness and making it difficult to see the pale eight-legged horse only a few feet ahead. As we emerge into the unknown, I grasp Elan's reins firmly, grateful for the security I feel while riding her enormous form.

Grunts and the scrapes of talons against wood confirm that Drogon, Tanda, and Naga have exited the world tree. As each dragon claws out of the trunk, short, sharp inhales escape the riders—Hildr, Britta, and Eir.

We follow Thor, who is riding Sleipnir. The irony isn't lost on me that another of Loki's children accompanies us as we seek his daughter. Despite having double the number of legs of an average horse, at least Sleipnir isn't a monster like Jormungandr, Fenrir, and Hel.

Strange noises sound as if they are close by, and the atmosphere turns spooky as wet fingers of mist spray across my skin. My neck and shoulders tingle, ridging my back in anticipation of the danger lurking in the darkness.

A slight breeze passes through my hair, dragging with it the stench of corpses. I screw up my nose and shift uncomfortably in my saddle. The cause of the offensive smell is near, if obscured by the lack of visibility. I'm on edge, and my fingernails dig into my palms as I sway with Elan's footsteps. I slip my hand under a golden scale, reaching for Elan's tender skin underneath. My vision connects to hers through our bond, only to be disappointed. Even the dragons can't see more than a few feet ahead. Elan's vision of the ground is clearer than mine, but as soon as she raises her head to see where she's going, her sight is severed by a dense wall of mist.

The cry of an eagle cuts through the veil. Its wail slices through my nerves as it repeats the cry, sounding as though it's circling above. When I crane my neck in an attempt to see, I'm met with the thick dome of mist.

I want to stretch my legs, I say down our bond, and

Elan crouches until her stomach rests on the ground. I grab the edges of her saddle and slide down.

Elan stands and nudges me with her nose. *Stay close.*

I grip the end of the lead, using it as a guide in the dark, making sure I always have contact with her. "I will." At first, my feet stumble in the dark, and I'm unable to see what I'm walking on. I persist, working out the cramps in the backs of my thighs from riding on the saddle for so long. Something rams me from behind, and I stumble.

"Sorry," Britta whispers, grasping my upper arms and bracing herself. "I can't see a thing."

"Me either," I whisper in return. "It's setting me on edge."

Rocks scatter on my right, and when I reach out, my hand brushes against hard scales. I sigh with relief, knowing it's one of our dragon friends.

It's just me.

I chuckle down our bond when I hear Elan's voice. *I'm glad. I'm a little bit jumpy.* I tighten my grasp on her rein, realizing it has slackened.

Aren't we all? Elan agrees.

Inching closer, I slip a hand under her scales, hoping that the way ahead has cleared.

It's no use trying to connect with my sight if that's what you're doing. She expels a long tendril of steam, briefly warming my right side. *This mist is stopping us from seeing anything. The four of us are just as blind as you are.* She snorts. *If only you knew how many times Drogon has rammed up my backside.*

What about Zildryss? Can he see anything? I continue our conversation through the merge of our minds.

Nope. He's just hanging on tight to my horns and riding like a king on top of my head.

I smile, even though I know nobody can see it. *And rightfully so.* The toe of my boot catches on something, and I stumble then take a few steps to right myself.

I think you should return to my back. With my four feet, I have better balance and coordination.

You're right. Shuffles beside me tell me that Elan has lowered to the ground, and I pull myself up by the edges of her saddle and coil the additional length of her lead. The steady sway of Elan's body works away the tightness in my muscles.

Sleipnir's hooves clop in front of me, the only indication that Thor is still ahead of us.

"Thor, are you sure we're in the right place?" Hildr calls from behind us.

My teeth clench, and I cringe at the loudness of her voice.

"I believe we are. Sleipnir gave me the impression

that this is the right exit. My father said the horse knows the way. Besides, Helheim is supposed to be dark, although I don't remember the description saying anything about all this mist." His confusion is evident in his voice. "And I expected to see more souls." He grunts. "I don't know. I've never been to Helheim before."

"Maybe we should go back to Yggdrasil and take a different exit," Britta suggests.

Thor's silence is broken by the clopping of Odin's eight-legged horse. The king of the gods lent it to his son, as he deemed it a faster mode of transport than Thor's carriage pulled by goats. The clopping stills as the horse stops, and Elan's pace slows.

"I don't know. Perhaps we should try another exit." Frustration fills the god's voice. "This one gives me a peculiar feeling, and it smells. I hope that this isn't where Balder ends up. That would be a sorrowful afterlife for someone as lovable as Balder."

A scream pierces the air, and a chill runs through my bones. It's not the same cry as that of an eagle. It sounds more sinister, like a human in distress. All feeling seeps from my limbs as the scream repeats, and I'm glad that Elan is beneath me, keeping me away from the unseen terrors of the ground.

"I vote we go back to the world tree." Britta's

panicked whisper edges through the darkness from behind. "This place is giving me the creeps."

Naga can smell the way back. Naga will lead the way. There's surprising strength in the smaller dragon's voice.

"Fantastic!" Hildr's gruff response is overenthusiastic. "That's wonderful, Naga! Lead the way."

The dragons about-face and follow Naga, each staying within a foot of the dragon in front, and Sleipnir, carrying Thor, trots alongside Elan's enormous back legs. More groans and screams pierce the air, increasing the urgency that we leave.

Elan groans. *I'd love to blast a plume of fire to light up the way and see if that helps us see through this mist, but I don't want to attract the attention of whatever it is out there.* Her body shivers underneath me, as though someone has just walked over her grave. *Judging by those screams, it doesn't sound like good news.*

I agree, I say through our bond. *That doesn't sound like a welcoming party.* I softly call over my shoulder, "Is this what you're expecting from the realm, Thor?"

"I wasn't sure what to expect. But I have a sneaking suspicion that this is Niflheim, not Helheim."

My brows pinch together. "What's the difference?"

"Have heard that Niflheim is cold and filled with mist and darkness. It's a place where all the evildoers go." Thor's voice wavers. He clears it, trying to keep it steady, but I hear the trace of uncertainty he attempts to hide.

I rub my upper arm to warm it against the chill. "What defines an evildoer?" Another scream sounds closer than the last, and I hug my chest.

Thor grunts. "It is all the murderers, rapists, dishonorable characters who purposefully make others suffer. They are stranded here, sent by Hel, and they are surrounded and trapped by the river Gjoll. At least that's what I'm led to believe, but I'm not sure. I haven't been there."

Great! Elan says. *Now my scales are definitely standing on end—not for me but for you five.*

"Why so?" I ask.

If they are murderers, I can only guess what seeing five live people would do to them. I imagine it would be too much temptation for them.

That simple statement puts us all on edge even further. No wonder the screams are so blood-chilling. As though on cue, another shriek rings out, and I'm astonished at how easily I can imagine it comes from someone being murdered. Even though they are in the depths of Niflheim, they continue to murder.

"What I don't understand is how people can be

murdered when they're already dead," Britta says, her voice only slightly louder than a whisper.

"Hmm. Good point." Thor's saddle creaks as he shifts. "I believe that they come down here and live like they're flesh and blood." He breathes in deeply and gags. "Maybe decaying flesh and blood, by that stench. This enables them to experience the sensation of living, yet at the same time, also the punishments or rewards for their past life."

We all fall into a silence broken only by the scraping of the dragons' talons on the rocks and the clopping of Sleipnir's hooves. Even these soft sounds are too loud for this realm, leaving us open to discoverability.

I spend the time pondering what Thor has said about the realm only to have my thoughts interrupted by Eir's elevated voice. "Ah, guys. We have a problem."

"What is it?" Thor asks as the clopping of hooves moves past the front of Elan.

"Naga has found the hole to the world tree, but it's blocked."

Naga can see into it, but it won't let Naga push through. Uncertainty taints Naga's voice. *It won't let us leave.*

"I've tried it too." Eir's voice is strained. "It appears we are stuck on this realm."

Chapter Two

"What?" Britta exclaims in a high-pitched whisper.

"As Naga said, the world tree is refusing to let us enter. We can see the hole but can't enter it," Eir says.

Elan moves toward Eir's voice, and I nervously twist the reins of her saddle around my fingers. "If what Thor says is true, we have come out of Yggdrasil into the wrong realm. This is probably Niflheim, and the tree allows us only to enter and not exit, as it is trapping the evildoers inside. In that case, we are stuck in the fail-safe against the evildoers' escape. It stops them from leaving this realm without any thought for people who enter by mistake."

"Yes, I would believe that so."

I jump at the sound of Thor's voice behind me. It is too dark and misty for me to see that Elan has passed him.

Another screech fills the air, this time accompanied by the sound of slicing through bone. "Oh, Vanir!" Hildr exclaims, followed by what sounds like metal sliding, indicating that she has drawn her sword. "That's too close for comfort."

"What are we going to do?" Britta asks.

"I'm afraid there's only one thing left to do," Thor says. The clopping of the horse's hooves approaches from behind Elan, and they're moving closer to the other dragons. "We're going to have to continue forward. There must be some way out of here other than through Yggdrasil. After all, I'm pretty sure this place is connected to Helheim somehow. This is the area where Hel discards murderers and thieves. It's their secluded section where they can wreak havoc amongst each other and not disturb the peaceful souls of Helheim."

There is a reluctance in Elan's footsteps as she turns around to head back toward where we came. *There's no way I'm letting you off my back*, she says. *You're staying on top.*

And why's that? I ask, continuing the conversation through our bond.

Because no murderers and thieves can reach you. I'll take them out before they even get close. Somehow, her voice sounds as though she has spoken through gritted teeth.

I guess you have a point. I slide a hand under a

scale just in front of the saddle and stroke the soft skin underneath, welcoming the warmth warding off the chilly mist that surrounds us. The gentle sway from Elan's footsteps lulls me with a false sense of peace in this dreadful realm, and I'm lulled further as the folds of her wings brush against my calves. Relishing the warmth created by my dragon friend, I'm reminded of my dragon-scale cloak and pull it out of the saddlebag. I thread my arms into the sleeves and pull the hood over my head. With the vast darkness in this realm, I doubt I will need the cloak for invisibility. Still, I welcome the protection against the other elements and the shelter from the wet tendrils of mist that slowly soak my leather Valkyrie uniform.

A cry of a different kind travels down to us, sounding much closer than the first time we heard the shrill of a bird. A swipe of cold air surges from above, and I gaze up, catching a glimpse of a massive eagle in the tiny break of mist. Another screech pierces the air, this time much lower than the first. I catch a glimpse of the fog being pushed aside for a moment, exposing an enormous eagle circling, its wingspan over six feet.

The eagle swoops, then when Elan tilts her face to the sky and growls, accelerates to a higher altitude.

Dragon scales! I hate bottom-feeders. It was checking

us out to see if we're corpses. I had to let it know we weren't going down without a fight.

Unable to see the eagle, I breathe a small sigh of relief. *I think it got your message, Elan. It seems to have backed off from us a little.*

My short-lived relief is pushed away when a cry from a man is followed by the sound of swords swiping through flesh. The cry that I know will disturb my sleep was much closer than the last.

"Are we moving closer to them? Or are they just murdering each other closer to us?" Britta asks.

Nobody answers as the mist thickens around us, making it almost impossible to see farther than our reach. The ground shakes, and I feel the tremors running through Elan's body. "That shaking reminds me of when we were in Svartalfheim and Nidhogg was chewing the roots of Yggdrasil," I muse. "This time, it didn't feel as scary as it did when we were trapped inside those caves."

"I should hope it's not as powerful down here," Thor says, his voice coming from somewhere in front. "This should be the bottom of the tree and a sturdier realm than the other worlds protruding from the branches."

"Does this mean that Ratatoskr is down here?" Hildr asks.

"I don't know." I tug at the edges of my dragon-scale cloak. "If what Alvis said was true, the squirrel is probably stirring up mischief with Nidhogg."

Thor clears his throat. "Nidhogg is supposed to be in the area with the murderers and thieves. I believe that Niflheim is based at the roots of Yggdrasil. That should be here somewhere if we are where I think we are. Stay on full alert, people."

A strange wariness fills Thor's voice, and I wish to see his face to decipher his emotions. If Thor is fearful, then we should be petrified.

Way to make us worry, Thor, Elan says. *If only we could get rid of this mist. It's proving difficult to see any sign of an exit from this realm.*

The clop of Sleipnir's eight hooves quickens and drowns out the soft scratching of the dragons' talons against the solid ground. The clopping seems to diminish into the distance, and I worry that Thor is heading too far ahead of the rest of the group. I prepare to speak to Elan through our bond, to tell her to hurry and catch up with him, when my thoughts are interrupted by a thump then a groan from the space where Thor has disappeared.

Trying to push down my panic, I call, "Thor? Are you okay?"

When he doesn't answer, my panic escalates, and the eerie darkness grows without the interruption of the god's voice.

Still waiting for an answer, I talk to Elan through our bond. *Can you see him?*

She groans. *I can't see anything. It's incredibly frustrating. I should be able to see in the dark.*

Scuffling sounds reach us from ahead, accompanied by a few grunts, thuds, and otherworldly noises that send a chill straight to my bones. Lightning forks the sky, and for a moment, it illuminates the area, shooting down to Thor's hammer. The lightning seems to light up the mist and gives it the appearance of thick fog, making it difficult to see anything. Yet I catch a glimpse of several figures slumping over Thor, pinning him to the ground. His legs and arms flail as he attempts to get up. He jerks his arm holding the hammer without much success. The people pinning him down are kneeling on top of his arm.

Lightning forks off the hammer's head, lighting up the area again, and the electricity shoots directly into one of the bodies. The man collapses to the ground, and Sleipnir dances around the outside of the commotion, eyes wide and lashing out with kicks whenever an evildoer gets too close. When another bolt shoots into the sky, he stomps his hooves before backing away from the attackers. During the several bursts of lightning, I count thirteen attackers. With each one who is fended off or wounded to incapability, a replacement comes. The numbers are slowly diminishing to ten. The numbers may be small, yet they attack with more ferocity. I direct Elan toward Thor, only to lose my way as the sky falls dark and lightning ceases to ignite the sky. With the darkness, terror settles deep into my core as I fear for my leader.

Chapter Three

"Summon more lightning," I call to Thor. "That way, I can see you long enough to help." Despite my voice being loud, Thor doesn't answer. I grit my teeth out of nervousness for my leader. The rapid clopping of horse's hooves diminishes into the distance, and my blood freezes. Sleipnir must have abandoned him.

"Elan. We have to save him!" I yell, silently cursing the darkness shrouding our vision.

I'm trying, but I can't see him. She stomps her feet. *I could charge in that direction, but I'm too afraid I'll stomp on him and cause more damage.*

Drogon snorts. *Let me ram them all. I've got the horns to do it.*

The furrowing of my forehead causes my head to ache. "Elan's right. You can't, Drogon. You might tread on Thor. He's pinned under all those dead people."

"What are we going to do?" Eir's soft voice meets me through the darkness.

"I've got an idea." Hildr sounds as though she is next to me, making it appear that Drogon has carried her closer.

"What's that?" I ask, but she doesn't answer.

Quietness lingers for a moment before it's interrupted by the strange grumblings of dead people. A giant *whoosh* flicks my hair across my face, followed by more grunts and groans and the sounds of people stumbling over each other as they try to secure their positions.

Hands clap beside me.

"I think that worked," Hildr says.

"What did you do?" I ask.

"I sent a ball of magic at them. It should have glided over the top of Thor." Hildr sighs. "I wish we could see."

"Thor, can you spark some lightning?" I ask.

In the quiet, as I wait for Thor's response, the discomfort of my soaked uniform begins to niggle at the back of my mind. The sleek layer of mist has finally seeped through the leather. Through the gap in the cloak, I run a hand down my pants and screw my nose in disgust.

A large groan that sounds like Thor comes from in

front of us, and in moments, he sends bolts of lightning into the sky.

Elan moves toward him, and I point at where the lightning split the darkness as though the others can see my motion. "He's over there."

Another bolt lights up the sky, showing the redheaded god within the gap between two mountains. My hope of finding Thor and moving on is smashed when I make out through the mist a crowd of pale-faced people circling the redheaded Thor. Sleipnir is nowhere to be seen, confirming my earlier assumption that he had run away.

"They must be going for Thor because he's on the ground," Britta calls.

Britta doesn't even finish her sentence before Elan charges forward, aiming for the last spot where the lightning left the ground. After several hurried footsteps, she comes to a sudden halt.

What's wrong? I ask.

I'm colliding into all these beings and stomping on them as I pass.

I frown. *Isn't that good?*

Kind of, she says hesitantly. *Except I've lost track of exactly where Thor will be. I'm afraid that I might run over him.*

I see your point. "Thor, can you send out another bolt of lightning?"

A grunt stemming from the extensive effort barely reaches me before lightning cracks and hits the sky. A scream pierces the air, and I jump.

Naga wails, *They're attacking Naga and Eir!*

And us too, Tanda cries. *They're pulling Britta off my back.*

Another crack of lightning shoots into the sky, and something lands on top of me, hooking on to my cloak and dragging me from Elan's back. They must have jumped from the top of one of the mountains. The attacker pulls the wrist of my coat sleeve, and it slips off my arm. I flick my arm away from the attacker and tighten my grip around the saddle's straps, desperate to cling on. Something cold and slimy grabs me from behind, leaning over my back, hooking a mucky arm around my neck, and dragging me backward. A tiny squeak pierces the air, and I realize Zildryss is also panicking.

With my voice box getting crushed, I speak down our bond. *Elan! Something's got me and is trying to drag me off your back.*

Elan flips in an attempt to pull me in the opposite direction, and I lose traction, my hands slipping down the leather of the saddle. The movement drags the coat right off my body as I descend. I grab purchase on the reins and dangle down her flank, trying to find a toehold or a stirrup to hook my boots into.

Hang on! Elan screeches.

Grunts and groans make it sound like Thor isn't far away. It sounds as though he is still fighting the attackers. I long to help him, but right now, I have myself to worry about. Although I try desperately to wrap my fingers around the strap and pull myself up, I fail. They slip farther down the reins, and the strap burns my palms and cuts into my fingers as someone grabs me from behind, adding extra weight to my clasp.

I kick out, trying to dislodge whoever is dragging me down. My foot connects with something that feels like flesh. Inwardly, I cheer and reward my effort with another mighty kick at the assailant.

Nails scratch my uniform as the attacker slips farther down my body. I'm almost ready to kick the attacker off their final hold when I'm grasped from another angle by a different assailant, the additional weight dragging me toward the ground, the reins cutting deeper into my palms. To make matters worse, we are weighted down again as another evil-doer slides along Elan's back, pulling me closer to the ground, and then comes another one. Warm blood oozes over my palms from the cuts, making it harder to grip the reins.

Get off! Elan growls.

The weight pulling me down grows lighter, only to be replaced by another sudden pressure and a thickening stench of rotting corpses.

Argh! I'm trying to pull them off, but more keep coming, Elan cries. *Hang in there and keep fighting.*

I kick again, but somehow, I miss. For people who are dead, these evildoers are indeed fast. Pulling strength from my core, I thrash, cringing from the pain caused by the cuts on my hand, and I kick again. My foot collides with flesh, but it doesn't budge. I can't seem to kick these last ones off.

Another attacker slides down the reins until they almost sit on my head. A stench smothers my face and cuts off my oxygen, making it practically impossible to catch a breath. Slimy flesh wraps around my neck, and I don't want to know what is pressing up against my face. I want to gag and cry out but can't. My mouth is sealed. It makes sense now that Thor didn't cry out to us. He probably had something similar happen to him.

I feel Elan is still trying to help me. She rips at the evildoers with talons and teeth in an attempt to get them off me. Yet for each one she removes, another one, if not two, seems to take its place. Her back must be covered in them.

The reins cut deeper into my palms as they slip

over my blood, and I let go. I can't defend myself like this. I need my arms to be able to fight better. My feet slide to the ground with a thud, and arms grab me from all directions. Spinning, I shoot magic into anybody who lays a hand on me, continuing my defense when another attacker replaces the one who fell away.

The cycle continues. I'm constantly surrounded and mauled, fighting them off with magic and battle skills. More desperate souls clasp on to me, their numbers growing. Each one I fight off weakens me more until I'm dragged down, pinned to the ground.

Almost depleted of energy, I grasp the pendant on my necklace, using the magic stored within, and shoot several more forms. Still, the effect doesn't last long. All of my magic and energy is depleting. I have no idea why these desperate souls are dragging Thor and me down, and I have no idea what is happening to the other Valkyries. We are all trained fighters but handicapped by the inability to see, and there are too many of the evildoers.

An almighty thud sounds above me, and the weight of several forms suddenly lifts. Another thud sounds over the top, accompanying the large dragon's tail gliding a foot above me. Elan is whacking them to the side.

Elan roars. *I want to burn them, but I'm afraid I'll*

hurt one of us instead. Nothing else I do seems to deter these filthy creatures.

I manage to push off a hand, covering my mouth, then spit out dirt and whatever else coats the skin while I shove them higher. "Whip your tail again, Elan!" Instantly, her long tail glides over the top of me, whacking aside the attacking bodies.

My relief is short-lived as more smelly figures squat over me, pinning me onto my back with their knees. My lungs burn from lack of breath as I struggle to free myself. Each figure I touch, I assault with aggressive magic, but each blast grows weaker as my energy diminishes.

Another large, slimy hand—again stinking of corpses—clasps my mouth and nose. I jerk up my knee and twist, struggling to land a kick onto these lowlifes mauling me. I attempt to call the others the second my mouth is free from the latest grasp, but my effort is a muffled cry.

A roar sounding like Drogon rises above the primal mauling noises our attackers expel, and I get the impression that Hildr is facing the same fate as me.

I thrash some more. This isn't the way we are going to leave this world. *Elan, can you swipe your tail again?* Once again, I'm thankful I can speak to her through our bond. Almost instantly, my attackers are wiped aside again, and a whoosh of air chills my wet skin. I scramble to my feet and get onto my knees only to be wrestled to the ground again.

Are you serious? I cry through mind speak. *Will these things ever stop coming?*

The other dragons have informed me that they're having the same trouble. I can't see enough to grab them off you. Can you call out loud so I can hear where you are?

That's going to be difficult. They seem to like covering my mouth all the time.

Dragon scales! That's inconvenient. Next time your mouth is free, yell out, and I'll follow the sound. She lets out a loud grunt. *They're certainly persistent. I'm also dragging them off myself. For some reason, they think they can take the dragons down too. Idiots! Unless they have a secret weapon, I don't know how they think that will happen.* She grunts a couple of more times. *We need to be connected with our riders and Thor again so we can get out of here, but we can't see any of you. That means that we need you lot to make some noise.*

I'll do my best. I can't see anything either. I can barely see these things in front of me, and making matters worse, my magic is depleted. I'm almost entirely out of energy.

Despite that, I'm not giving up. I wriggle and squirm under these figures in my last attempts to release their hold over me. It's hard to believe that beings who are supposed to be dead are so strong.

It's almost as though they have supernatural powers. Thrashing my head from side to side, I cry over our bond. *I'm trying, Elan. I just can't seem to get them off my mouth. The second I get it free long enough to take a breath to yell, it's covered again.*

Try harder. Her words sound like they're being said through gritted teeth, and she follows them with a roar filled with despair. *Oh, dragon scales!*

What is it? I stop struggling.

Defeat and worry seep through her words. *Zildryss is gone.*

Chapter Four

My heart skips a beat. Tiny Zildryss is gone. It's not bad enough that the Valkyries and Thor are in trouble from these beings attacking us. I can't bear to think of him defending himself against these terrible creatures.

Oh. That's not good, Elan. I thrash out at another attacker with my leg and pant through my nose. *Have you tried calling out to him?*

Of course I have, she snaps. *It's not as though he talks. He's only into showing pictures.*

The thought of the tiny dragon out there under attack gives me another burst of adrenaline, and I twist my body and swipe my arm, knocking the hand of one of the attackers. I cry out with disappointment when a slimy hand instantly covers my mouth again, stealing my tiny burst of energy.

I groan. *I'm so tired, Elan!*

Don't you dare give up fighting. You hear me?

Yes. I hear you. Still, I don't think I can keep this up for much longer. I don't think I have ever felt this worn out.

We're going to get you out of here, and we're going to help the others. Let me know when I can swipe my tail again.

Go for it! It's not like I'm getting up anytime soon.

She swings her tail, knocking many of the attackers off, but one stays low, crouching over the top of me, and her attack glides above me.

Otherworldly noises surround me, and I groan in defeat. *One of them has worked out what we're doing, and they've remained under your swipe.*

The male lowers his face to just above mine, and the sickly smell radiating off him is overpowering. I want to gag, but I can't even find enough energy to remove his hand from my mouth.

My arms flop, lifeless by my side. Every single muscle in my body is exhausted and crying out in pain from the exertion. *I didn't think this would be how I would go, Elan. But I just want you to know, it's been lovely having you as my friend.*

Don't you dare give up. You aren't going to be dying here, especially not right now, and you are certainly not going to live here. You just need to get your mouth free so that you can yell your position, and I'll come grab you.

Despite my predicament, I huff. *I'm not going to be*

living here. I wouldn't class myself as a murderer or a thief, nor do I have any of the dishonorable traits that would land someone here.

The rip of fabric followed by a cold chill tells me my uniform is severed, leaving a gaping hole over my abdomen. An involuntary shiver rocks my spine. These are murderers, rapists, and other unsavory characters. I dread to think of what their sick, perverted minds have planned for me or the other Valkyries.

My uniform rips some more, and cold air brushes against my hip. I struggle, arching my back and thrashing my hips. My arms are released briefly, and I elbow the face towering over me—all with minimal effect. More beings pin me down, and I use the last of my strength to fight, reminding myself that I am a Valkyrie, and we don't go down easily.

A mighty roar cuts through the unearthly noise these creatures are making, and I know it isn't one of our dragons. My cheeks turn clammy. Even the evil-doers stop their attack momentarily, their bodies stiffening.

I turn their hesitation to my advantage and lash out, releasing an arm and punching my forefront attacker in the jaw. The man lurches to the side, removing some of his weight from my torso. I scramble to my side, aiding his fall before clambering to all fours. Somehow, this seems to spark the attackers in the background to life, and they return their attention to me with brutal force.

I'm slammed from the side so hard that it feels like a dragon has hit me. Yet even in the dark, I know it isn't one of my friends. They wouldn't pin me on my back and treat me the way this creature does. Once again, my arms and legs are pinned to the ground by what feels like one person per limb. I wish this mist and darkness would go away so that we could fight these attackers in unison.

Another mighty roar fills the darkness, this time much closer than the last. My eyes widen, and I attempt to fight against the darkness to see what kind of creature it is. If it's also after us, we don't have a chance, especially if it can see us through the dark. Worrying about what the creature might do to us gnaws into my strength, but then, I would rather be chewed by a giant animal than die at the hands of these evildoers. At the creature's third roar, I realize it is much closer, and our attackers are distracted longer.

After much thrashing, I headbutt the closest attacker and tip the others off then scramble to my hands and knees. It takes only a moment before they're climbing all over my back, pulling my feet backward and pressing me to the ground and onto my stomach. Through my leather uniform, rocks scrape my knees, and I grit my teeth when they knock against my bones. I choke back a cry of pain when a larger rock lodges under my stomach and hips as my attackers sit on my back, pressing me face-first into the ground.

After it gives another roar, I'm convinced the mysterious creature is only a few feet away. Whatever it is, it's definitely close. The attackers on my back hold still as though in a weak attempt to hide from the creature. The ground shakes to the tune of giant footsteps, and the earth trembles under my stomach. I wish I knew what kind of creature is tromping around. Still, I think if there is a choice between leaving this life by either the beast or these evildoers attacking me, the beast would be my preferred method.

A new chorus of cries rings out, and they sound like they're coming from our attackers. The tearing of flesh and chomping of bones brings a mixture of joy and the urge to hurl when another of our attackers is attacked. The sound of a large tongue smacking against lavish lips brings delight then apprehension when I remind myself that this creature could do the same to my friends and me. I'm not sure whether I should stay put or scurry away. To where? I don't know.

The darkness and mist make it impossible to see much farther than arms reach. The weight of my attackers lightens one by one, becoming nonexistent when the final attacker pinning me down is ripped away.

A presence shifts above me, and I curl into a fetal position. The ground shakes violently, and I sense the presence of large legs on all sides, holding the looming creature above. I hug my legs tighter, hoping the beast doesn't walk on me or isn't searching for my flesh. I wouldn't have a chance fighting it on my own, even with magic.

When I sense its presence moving, relief floods my body. A steady pace of thunderous footsteps treads around me then slowly goes away. My heart thunders and skips a beat when the strangled cries of terror, not from my companions, are quickly cut short.

Warm, smelly liquid showers over me and trickles down my sides, and my nose screws in disgust. The crunching and slurping sounds of the creature eating the murderers and thieves is repulsive enough but having their corpse-smelling blood drizzling over me takes "nauseating" to another level.

An unexpected voice causes me to jump.

"We have guests." A strong lisp alters the words, and the structure of the voice and words sounds strangely immature. "You don't treat guests like this."

The terrifying roar sounds odd after the voice, yet something tells me it's from the same creature, the attacker of our attackers. "Murderous, vile creatures." The ground thunders again and shakes in time to giant footsteps as the creature crawls over me. Something brushes against my skin, and I jump. Scaly, lizard-like skin, similar to that of a snake, strokes my exposed flesh. Unlike the cold-bloodedness of a snake, however, this creature is warm even though the environment is cold. Daring myself to be brave, I rest my hand on something that feels like a tail as it slithers past until the tip passes. Another scream from the direction it headed has me jumping again.

Realizing the creature isn't going to eat me, I slowly rise to my hands and knees then brush down my uniform and rub several sore spots before wiping the smelly blood from my face with my sleeve. My bones ache, and my muscles scream their protest over the many recently inflicted bruises covering my body. Trying to loosen up, I rock on all fours then freeze when something clambers up my arm and circles around my neck before sitting on my shoulder.

"Zildryss?"

Relief oozes from my pores when the tiny dragon presses against the flesh of my neck and projects images into my mind, confirming it is him. He shows me a picture of him flying alone in the darkness as he searches the world tree's roots and comes across a creature similar to a dragon but with only two rear feet and the front arms attached to the wings. It's a wyvern. I thought they were extinct. Zildryss shows the wyvern eating the roots of Yggdrasil, instantly connecting the wyvern to Nidhogg. I can't help worrying for the little dragon as he shows me how he approaches the wyvern and asks for his help. I'm astounded when Nidhogg agrees without a moment's hesitation.

"You don't treat our guests like this," Nidhogg says again, interrupting Zildryss's explanation, followed by several quick, thunderous stomps.

"Thank you, Zildryss." I rest my hand over his tiny body, and he nestles his head into my palm. The movement places pressure on my recent injuries, but I ignore the unintended pain. "You had us worried. We thought you were hurt and lost to us forever. Instead, once again, you're coming to our rescue." Climbing to my feet, I call to Elan through our bond. *Are you okay?*

Of course I'm okay. Are you? Warmth fills my insides. Elan sounds unharmed and probably more

33

concerned about me. *You sound almost relaxed. Aren't you afraid of the creature?*

I shake my head before realizing no one can see me. *No. Apparently, the creature is Nidhogg, and he's here to protect us. Zildryss found him and asked for him to help. He's back and sitting on my shoulder.*

She huffs down our bond. *That adorable, talented little dragon. Always full of surprises.*

He sure is. Another scream cuts through the air, and I push away the shivers arising from the terror and search for the others. "Thor! Are you okay?"

Thor groans loudly. "I'm battered and bruised but otherwise fine. Probably my pride hurts more than anything else. I thought Svartalfheim was unwelcoming, but I think this one wins."

"Not all of us are unfriendly. I'll welcome you," Nidhogg lisps. "I'm Nidhogg. It's nice to have real guests for a change. It's a pleasant break from being surrounded by those murderous thieves."

"Thanks, Nidhogg," Thor groans. "We appreciate your help."

Nidhogg chuckles and almost sounds shy. "My pleasure. You will be safe from the evildoers for a while now."

"Fantastic. Thanks." Thor sounds genuinely appreciative.

"Is everyone else okay?" I ask. Their silence makes me worry.

I almost cry with relief when I hear everyone's delayed response. They sound battered and bruised but alive and no longer threatened.

Chapter Five

Something oozes down my back, and I cringe. Holding on to the hope that it may just be Nidhogg's drool, I touch the reachable parts of my back and come away with goop-covered hands. The stench of rotting corpses curls my lips and makes me want to vomit. I flick my fingers frantically, trying to remove the goo from my skin. I have never felt something so disgusting, and knowing it's leftovers from the evildoers that Nidhogg attacked makes it worse.

More chomping, stomping, and tearing of flesh draws my attention long enough for me to cringe at the destruction the wyvern is creating. There must be remaining attackers lurking in the fog. Zildryss wriggles, filling my mind with images of my companions and taking my thoughts to a happier place. Knowing that the little dragon had found his way back to us fills me with the hope that they, too, remain okay. The sound of Nidhogg warding off our attackers lingers, but this doesn't put me off. I need to reach out to my friends.

"Is everyone okay?" I check again keeping my voice at a normal level and clench my teeth as another scream pierces the air.

Slowly, each of my friends answers, followed by their dragons, their combined voices shifting closer with every call until eventually, we're within arm's reach of each other. The Valkyries and Thor have dark patches over their skin—they're also covered in the evildoers' blood. Knowing it isn't their blood brings me some relief, yet they also exhibit swollen eyes and jaws and cuts tracking across any exposed skin. They appear as battered as I feel and probably look.

A whoosh of wings swishes pebbles and dust around us, catching in our eyes. As I blink, attempting to clear the dirt away, I catch sight of softer scales swirling around our little group, and legs smaller than those of our dragons.

An eagle cries as it soars above us, chased by a bellowing roar, and despite knowing that Nidhogg is our friend, I can't help cringing.

With his face tilted to the sky, Nidhogg yells at the eagle, outlined briefly by the fiery glow of Helheim, "Get away from my guests, Hraevelg!"

I struggle to get used to the lisp and, for a

moment, wonder why he speaks like this. Then it dawns on me. He's speaking out loud. Our dragons speak to us internally, so we wouldn't know if they spoke with a lisp or not. "These are not for you to eat. They're far from rotting corpses. Go and find one of the evildoers."

Nidhogg roars again from deep within his gut. A shadow casts across us as he towers protectively. We have done nothing to deserve his protection, and I can't help wondering why he is doing this.

When the threat leaves, Nidhogg stands next to the other dragons. His dim outline in the darkness displays how much shorter he is compared to his cousins. "You lot have landed in the wrong part of this world. What brings you down here?"

Thor runs a hand over his face and through his matted hair. "We're looking for Hel. My brother, Balder, had an unfortunate death and didn't die during a battle. Because of this, he would have been sent down here. He was a good man. He doesn't deserve to live with dishonor. We have come to ask Hel to release him. So many people mourn him."

Nidhogg blows a giant raspberry. "Good luck with that. Hel doesn't release anybody." He tilts his head to one side, exposing more of his long, thin neck. "Even so, you have definitely landed in the wrong part of the realm. This is Niflheim. This isn't where someone like your brother would end up. This consists only of evildoers, murderers, the deceivers—those who've committed the worst crimes of the realms."

Thor huffs, clearly frustrated. "Not long after we left Yggdrasil, we realized we must've been in the wrong place, but we couldn't get back into the trunk to travel to Helheim."

Nidhogg chuckles. "Yes, that's right. That's to stop the evildoers from escaping and entering the other worlds."

Britta ties her blood-soaked hair into a ponytail, her face cringing as if she's disgusted. "Then how do we leave?"

Tanda levels her gaze to us. "If we could see farther than our noses, we could fly you out."

Nidhogg scoffs. "That's not going to happen."

"And why not?" Hildr scowls. "Isn't Helheim the same level as Niflheim?"

Nidhogg nods.

Hildr places a hand on Drogon's front leg. "Then we have dragons with perfectly good wings. They could easily fly us out of here."

Nidhogg holds up his front arms and spreads his wings. "I have perfectly good wings also. I can fly, but I can't leave here without approval."

Eir blinks and wipes her face with a sleeve. "Why not?"

"Here. Let me show you." Nidhogg turns in the opposite direction and slaps his tail in the middle of our tight circle. "Grab on to my tail. I have the ability to see through this fog, and I can guide you."

Elan squats into the position where I can climb on. "First, let our riders sit on our backs. The dragons will join together by grabbing the tail in front, and you can lead the way." She nudges Thor. "I guess you can hop onto my back too. It's clear Sleipnir isn't coming back anytime soon."

Thor stands near her side without wasting a beat, clearly preparing to launch up using the stirrups. "Much obliged."

Elan lowers farther, and I yank on the saddle before pulling myself up and flipping one leg over the top. Then I reach down and lend Thor a hand.

Elan flicks her head, and something hits me on the leg. *Here. I found this on the ground.*

Grabbing the item, I almost squeal with delight when the rough scales dig into my hands. It's my dragon-scale cloak. I had forgotten about it in my fight for survival. After giving it a quick hug, I tuck it away into the saddle pouch and clasp the reins.

Thor grabs my waist, and Elan rises to her feet as the other riders groan and climb onto their dragons.

Undoubtedly, their bodies are as battered and bruised as mine.

The friendly lisp of Nidhogg calls from in front. "Okay. Everyone is grabbing each other's tails. Let's go!"

The trek takes us through dark valleys and up high mountains, yet the thick layers of fog restrict our vision. I am all too aware of my torn, blood-soaked uniform. In many ways, I wish it would rain to wash away the filth.

The coolness of the realm adds to my discomfort. The large tear in my uniform leaves a lot of flesh exposed, and each puff of breeze raises hundreds of goose bumps. I long to change into my fresh uniform in my pack, but I wouldn't feel much better because of the muck caked on my body.

Eventually, the mist thins, and Nidhogg leads us into a clearing, with visibility being more than a couple of feet in front of us. Large tree roots tower over the clearing, and a raised pool lies at the end of a root to the side, barely within view. Despite the area still being dark and gloomy and a thick fog encasing it, it has a strange, cozy feel.

A horse canters across the opening and rises, kicking into the air.

"Sleipnir!" Thor calls. "Am I glad to see you! I

thought I'd lost you forever." He scurries off Elan's back and approaches the horse.

Elan releases Nidhogg's tail, and the dragons line up in the inner circle of the mist. Now that the fog is not shrouding everything, Nidhogg is easier to see. Two horns stick out of the crown of his head, curving slightly toward each other. He has a strangely long body in comparison to the dragons. His form reminds me of a snake except for the addition of legs —two short ones at the front attached to wings, and two larger back legs to walk on.

Nidhogg waves his front arms, exposing his membranous wings as he indicates the opening. "This is my private area and where I spend most of my time. There's a fresh well where you can clean up at the boot of Yggdrasil's root over there."

I eye the pool, a deep longing to dive in rising to the surface.

Watching my face, Nidhogg continues, "I can see you're covered in filth. You must be longing to wash up and change. Do you have spare clothes?"

"Oh, we do," Britta says. Her desire sounds as deep as mine feels.

I disembark Elan's back, grab a fresh uniform, and race to the water's edge. The pool is a strange formation for a natural pond. It is almost like the water is sitting above ground in a large bowl. After placing my fresh uniform on the side of the pool, I dip my fingers into the water then retract them quickly. The water is icy cold. Taking one look at my filthy torn uniform, I grit my teeth and climb in, ignoring my muscles' protest until they adapt to the cold. Once in the pool, I use my magic to heat the water immediately around me, strip off my old uniform, dump it over the edge, and wave my arms in cool water, warming slowly as I heat it with my magic. It is indeed fresh water, and I'm happy to be the first to wash away my filth and grime.

Elan moves to stand guard near the pool to protect me from any evildoers and block the view of others while I scrub every inch of my flesh.

When finished, I climb out and change behind the raised edges of the pool. By the time I'm through, the other three Valkyries have climbed in together, and when they have finished, Thor follows them. Thor doesn't have a change of clothes, so after he's finished scrubbing his old ones clean, the dragons dry his clothes with the heat from their fires. When he has finished, it is almost comical seeing the dragons try to wash up two at a time. They barely fit in the pool.

Nidhogg lights a small fire in the clearing's center, and the Valkyries and Thor gather around it, soaking up the heat. The fire illuminates Nidhogg's scaly skin, highlighting green stripes on his medium-brown body.

Elan collapses beside me. *Ah. That feels better.* Her scales are glowing a deep gold in the light of the fire.

"It sure does." I smile. Zildryss is sitting on top of Elan's head again, grabbing her horns. "Are you the king of dragons, Zildryss? You seem to like being perched on top of Elan's head like it's your throne."

The little dragon straightens his spine, looking pleased with himself.

Elan turns her eyes upward as though trying to spot the little dragon. "I would love to know how you knew how to find Nidhogg."

Her facial expression stills for a moment as he shows her in her mind.

"Oh. You could smell him." Elan twists her nose to the side. "You must have a strong nose, little guy. Especially if you can smell past the scent of corpses."

Zildryss screws up his nose and sticks out his tongue in an exaggerated split. "Argh."

A strange gnawing pulls my attention from the little dragon, and I find Nidhogg chewing at the roots of the world tree.

With my arms out and palms up, I charge over. "No! Please stop!"

Chapter Six

Nidhogg stops chewing on Yggdrasil's root and stares at me with a dumbfounded expression. "I have to gnaw at the root. The eagle just sent another insulting message through Ratatoskr, and it's the only way I can get my revenge. The bird sits at the peak of Yggdrasil's branches, sending me insults, and I'm stuck in Niflheim. One day, I'm going to knock it from the top."

"But don't you see? When you gnaw at the roots, you rattle the whole world tree, which shakes the other worlds." I indicate the top of the towering Yggdrasil. "You're causing things like earthquakes to happen in the other worlds, and I've been in some of those underground, and they're scary."

Nidhogg frowns. "But Ratatoskr has given me a message. I tell you, what that eagle says to me is disgusting."

After moving closer, I place a hand on his cheek.

"You can't trust Ratatoskr. He enjoys putting people down and passing on insulting messages. In fact, he won't carry a message unless it includes an insult."

Nidhogg's eyes widen, and he shakes his head wildly. "No! I believe the eagle is rude. It thinks it's so high and mighty being on top of Yggdrasil. It has to be knocked down."

Flailing my arms, I exclaim, "But you're destroying the world tree." My eyes land on the large chunk taken out of the base. "You're killing the root. Every time you take out another chunk, it gives the tree less chance of survival. Don't you realize that if you kill Yggdrasil, then you kill the worlds connected to it?"

Nidhogg scoffs. "Rubbish! There is no way I can kill the whole tree that carries the Norse worlds."

Elan studies the spot with the gaping hole. *You might want to look a little closer at the damage you've caused, my friend.* With a front talon, she indicates the damage. *This area around your bite marks is drying out and rotting, and it runs down the remainder of the root. The root should be healthy and robust, especially if it's nourished by the evildoers' rotting flesh stuck on Niflheim.*

Nidhogg straightens his spine, making him seem taller, almost the height of Naga, and his muscles tense as though upset with Elan's reasoning.

Hildr studies the wyvern, then the damage he has caused to the root, and crosses her arms. "This has me wondering. Perhaps Ratatoskr is trying to kill the world tree and bring down the worlds."

Eir stands on the other side of Hildr. "I hope not." She slides a hand over the rotting wood, and her eyes land on me. "Perhaps we can heal the tree."

I shrug. "We can only try. Maybe we can do some good while we're stuck down here."

Nidhogg moves away from the spot he was gnawing and slides off to the side on his stomach, giving us full access to the root.

"Maybe we can help." Britta places a hand on the root, and Hildr joins her. "We haven't had a chance to learn any of the magic you use that involves peace rather than destruction."

Zildryss flies off Elan's head, lands on Britta's shoulder, and presses his scales up against her neck. Her eyes turn blank then spark with intelligence.

"Ah. That seems so easy. Can you show Hildr as well?" She rubs the little dragon under the cheek, and he nods before flying to the redheaded Valkyrie. After the dragon instructs Hildr, the four of us place our hands on the damaged root and inject it with healing power. Slowly, the root is pushed aside by a fresh layer of green growth, healing the hole.

Britta pulls her hand away, smiling. "Perhaps that

will help save Yggdrasil and the attached worlds for a while."

Eir approaches Nidhogg and explains in her patient way, "Please remember that gnawing on this root is affecting the other worlds and damaging the world tree. I know that Ratatoskr brings you insults from the eagle, but there is no guarantee that these insults are true. The squirrel is full of mischief and loves to cause disruption. But please, remember the other worlds when you're taking anger out on the roots."

Nidhogg pulls up, making himself seem taller. "I can't make any promises. That eagle makes me so angry that I can't control myself."

Hildr's face distorts with obvious annoyance. "We can see that. I know what it's like to get angry, but you've got to control yourself, for the worlds' sake."

Screams sound in the distance, and Hildr's face pales in the dull light as her hand hovers over the hilt of her sword.

Nidhogg wraps his body around us protectively. "Relax. I've got your back. I'm not going to let them get you. However, I need to get you out of here. You don't belong." He stretches and poises his long body forward, pushes back and raises his backside into the air in a downward dog position, then rises to all fours. "Come on. You all look a bit better now. Let's get out of here before we get surrounded by more evildoers."

We climb onto our dragons' backs and Thor onto his father's horse, and we follow Nidhogg toward the outline of mist.

A nasal voice calls from the direction of the root, "Wait!"

The saddle squeaks as I gaze behind us to find the little red squirrel running down the newly healed root.

The rodent pauses at the green growth. "Wow! This is new." His voice is extra grating, giving me the urge to do something nasty, especially when he scratches the healed spot with his claws and sniffs it. "Definitely new—fresh and green." He brushes the scrapings out of his claws and against his white fur and stands straight. His beady eyes narrow on Thor before he glares at me, letting the hostility travel across our entourage. "What are you lot doing here?"

"I hope you haven't come to insult Nidhogg again so that he chews at the roots of the world tree." Even Eir's peaceful tone is laced with annoyance when speaking to the self-important messenger.

"Well, aren't we full of arrogance today?" Ratatoskr narrows his beady eyes at Eir. "In fact, I'm here to deliver a message from Loki."

"Oh." Thor pulls Sleipnir up in front of the squirrel, and the horse rears. "I hope he's enjoying his cell."

Ratatoskr points a claw at him and laughs, his other paw clasping his stomach as he rolls onto his back on the root. When he finally settles, he asks, "What cell? Do you honestly think Loki is still in the cell?" He cackles again and rolls a few more times on his back, stopping briefly to point at Thor before losing control again.

A bemused expression crosses Thor's face, awash with a ghostly white. "Why is that so funny? Loki is in his cell, isn't he?"

"Ohhh." Ratatoskr drags the word out. "Loki hasn't been in his cell for ages. He's the master of shape-shifting." His beady eyes glance over Sleipnir before returning to Thor. "Do you really think you can hold him in a cell? Why do you think his children are taking so long to attack when their one reason for it is that their father is captured?" the squirrel asks. "Jeez. You are loose a few screws, aren't you? Not quite a full lightning bolt, are you?"

Chapter Seven

My cheeks turn clammy, and I'm sure the color of my face matches Thor's. I dread thinking of the mischief Loki is getting up to if he can escape anytime he wants. "How is this time different from when he was tied up in the deep cave with venom dripping on him?"

Ratatoskr sighs as if impatient. "Ah. That held him better. The restraints had a magic that stopped his ability to shape-shift. This time, the fools only secured Loki in a normal cell. He can shape-shift and leave anytime he wants."

Thor's face distorts in obvious displeasure. "Noted. When we return, I shall have him secured properly."

Ratatoskr chuckles. "If you can find him. With your dim-witted intelligence, I doubt that would be quick."

Sitting on top of Elan, I'm almost at the same

height as the rodent as he remains on the world tree's root. I place my fists on my hips. "What is it that you want, Ratatoskr?"

He arches an eyebrow. "I told you. I have a message from Loki."

Drogon moves closer to the root, and Hildr glowers at the messenger. "Then give us the message and let us carry on with our business."

Ratatoskr wobbles his head. "Jeez. I see you haven't changed one bit, Hildr. You're just as charming as ever."

Elan positions me close to Hildr. "We all agree with Hildr. Pass on your so-called message from Loki and let us be on our way. We want to get our business done and get out of this world as soon as we can. It's not exactly the friendliest of places."

The rodent scoffs. "It seems like a lot of realms aren't offering you a friendly greeting these days. Isn't that telling you something?"

I light up a ball of magic on my palm and extend it threateningly toward him.

"All right, all right." He tosses a dismissive paw in my direction. "I'll pass on the message." He clears his throat and straightens his back. "Ahem. To my dim-witted relative"—Ratatoskr focuses on Thor —"and his trusted wingless Valkyries and their drag-ons." He eyes each one of us. "Loki wishes to tell you that if Frigg had kept her mouth shut about what could hurt Balder, you wouldn't be on this mission."

"Hey!" Thor blurts. "Don't you speak of my step-mother like that!"

Ratatoskr holds up his front foot. "Speak to the paw. I'm just passing on a message." He cups his jaw with a thumb and forefinger. "Now, where was I? Ah yes. If Frigg hadn't told the nice old lady, who was Loki in disguise, what would hurt Balder, then the old lady wouldn't have been able to give a spear fashioned from the unsworn mistletoe to Hodr. All the gods are so dim-witted that they didn't even know that Loki has shape-shifted into an old woman. She just had to whisper in the blind brother's ear what he could do to be included in the fun and games of throwing things at the invincible Balder. He said it was so easy to convince the stupid, dejected brother to throw that mistletoe spear straight at his brother's heart." Ratatoskr chuckles, and for a moment, it looks like Thor is about to throttle the squirrel. "Oh, the satisfaction Loki felt when Hodr did it."

His face red, Thor stomps toward the messenger. "Why would Loki do something like that?"

Ratatoskr taps his chin with his finger, looking pleased with himself. "Loki told me the reason. He was tired of Balder getting all the attention and ogling. The god of light had no trouble winning over everyone's hearts." He focuses on Britta. "No one should get that much attention from everyone. Besides, who does Frigg think she is to make everything in the universe swear not to harm her son just because he had some bad dreams? That's pathetic."

"That's not pathetic!" Thor thunders. "Balder was a decent person and worth saving. He's one of the most decent people I know. He deserved all that protection, and everything in this universe does love him."

Ratatoskr tuts. "But clearly not the mistletoe." He dusts his paws on the white fur of his chest.

Thor's face turns icy. "Is that it?"

Ratatoskr screws his mouth to one side. "I believe so. Now, do you have a returning insult for me to send?"

"Yeah," Thor says. "You tell that little god that I'm going to skin him alive when I find him. His daughter better release Balder from Helheim or else."

Ratatoskr shrugs, his fur coat a dull red in the backlight of the realm. "They're big threats for a stupid god." He clambers over the newly healed root and pauses midway. "Oh yeah. Nidhogg, I have something to tell you. The eagle says that you are the stupidest creature in the world. Your brain is so tiny that you cannot find your massive nose." With that, Ratatoskr climbs the world tree.

"Oh, that little...!" Nidhogg screams, charging toward the root with a new ferocity.

Naga slowly approaches the gnawing wyvern's side, Eir still on his back. *Naga knows how you feel, Nidhogg. You're angry and upset. And this is the only way that you can release that tension.* The blue dragon moves and looks Nidhogg in the eye. *You need to ignore the nasty eagle. What he says to you isn't true. Naga knows that you have a big brain inside of your head. It's buried deep within your reptilian scales.*

The wyvern's mouth stops. "Do you really think so?" Hope lurks within his lisp.

Naga nods. *Naga really does believe so.*

Nidhogg's shoulders slump, and he drops to the ground. "Oh, okay. I was going to show you out of here anyway." He makes his way back to where we were going to exit before we were interrupted by Ratatoskr then turns his attention to Naga. "I hope you're ready for this. This is going to be an interesting part. Modgud might not let you cross the bridge. I hope for your sake she does, as it's the only way out. I can't help you. Only you can get past her."

Naga stretches his wings out to the side, exposing the white stars underneath, and wraps them around the wyvern's shoulders. *We just need you to get us there, and we will work it out. This group has a good heart. Surely that can help.*

"I don't know. I've never had visitors before. You're the first, and you're the only ones who have tried to escape this area into Helheim. All the others here don't have a chance. They're evildoers, and they are banished to this area forever to become my tasty treats." He licks his lips lavishly, exposing his sharp, pointy teeth.

Yuck. Elan's voice sounds in my head. *That's disgusting.*

Chapter Eight

We follow Nidhogg through the mist. Although the fog eventually subsides enough for us to see several feet ahead, it hovers like draping blankets around the edges, thick and menacing. The chill remains, raising goose bumps under our damp leather uniforms. At least now, it's only water, not the blood of the evildoers.

We weave through mountains towering ominously over us, tension mounting as we pass every potential hiding place. Cries of the evildoers reach out to us near and far, adding to the eeriness and sending chills deep into our bones.

This is not how I pictured the afterlife to be. I speak to Elan across our bond.

Me neither, she agrees. *It's like they are dead and smell dead, yet they can still murder and continue to commit crimes or be destroyed. Life would be miserable.*

I continue to sway with the pacing of her footsteps, contemplating the life these people live. I can't get my mind past the devastation of it all and how dangerous it would be to live here. *I'm grateful that Nidhogg has taken it upon himself to protect us and lead us to the bridge.*

Naga walks beside Elan with Eir on his back. Even in the darkness, her deep shivers are visible every time a scream assaults our ears.

"I can't wait to get out of here," Eir mutters softly when another bone-chilling shrill rings out.

I wish I could remove the distress from her face. It's not like her to look so worried, and she is also a Valkyrie, but the attack earlier was disconcerting. "I agree. It's like these evildoers just won't stop trying to commit murder and evil against one another."

You don't need to worry, Eir. Naga's big blue eyes connect with mine before eyeing Elan. *Naga can protect you, and Naga's sure Elan will too.*

There is no hesitation in Elan's voice. *Absolutely. In fact, I'm sure all the dragons will protect every rider here. We just had trouble before because we couldn't see a thing. And now we have Nidhogg on our side.*

"But what happens if we're shrouded in mist again?" Eir asks.

Naga straightens and looks confident. *Then I'm sure Nidhogg will see through the mist, using his smell to track down the corpses and defend us. His sense of smell is much better than mine.*

I lower my voice. "That's a lot of trust to give someone we've just met. It's going to take more than one rescue for me to trust him completely."

Zildryss chirps, runs down Elan's neck, and crawls up my arm and over my shoulder until he touches the skin around my neck. Images bombard my thoughts, and I know that the little dragon is communicating with me. He shows me Nidhogg many times defending us, making our safety his top priority. Through the images, I can tell that he is far from the most intelligent, especially when it comes to the eagle on top of Yggdrasil, but his intentions are good. He doesn't tolerate the crimes of the evildoers, which is why he's patrolling the realm of Niflheim.

I stroke the little dragon's scales. "If what Zildryss has shown us is true, we can trust Nidhogg." Kinking my neck, I stare down at the little dragon. "I wish I knew how you know this, Zildryss. You are full of surprises."

With wide eyes, the lilac dragon stares up at me, his tongue swiping one eye then the other, his mouth seemingly curved in a smile. More screams surround us as we travel in wary silence. Occasionally, we catch glimpses of disheveled figures emerging from the fog ahead. They are scared away by Nidhogg's snapping jaws. Still, the number of times they appear increases as we progress.

Hildr catches up and walks with Drogon on my left side. "They seem to be closing in on us." Her hand braces her sword hilt, and considering her otherwise calm exterior, the gesture betrays her fear. Her hand always hovers over a sword when she's nervous.

I will kill them all. Drogon thrashes his multi-horned brown head from side to side. *I will ram these horns into their stomachs and fling them aside.*

Hildr slides a hand under his scales. "That you will, Drogon. Don't forget, in addition to these horns that many dragons would envy, you have a fantastic tail that works like a morning star. Then after you're done, you will fly high and glide over your victory unlike any other dragons."

Even though I know it's true, and I've studied his different form hundreds of times, I take in how Hildr's saddle sits farther forward than the rest of ours, and Drogon's unusual wings are fixed to the underside of his arms and the side of his torso. It gives him the perfect form to glide like a bat. Although Drogon's figure is different, all of the various breeds of dragons have some feature that makes them distinct from the others, despite their color.

A sudden jerk pulls my attention away from studying Drogon, and Elan blasts a plume of fire in a semicircle. Briefly, I catch sight of figures retreating into the fog. The muscles tighten on all four large dragons as they ready themselves for the next attack.

When Nidhogg realizes what Elan is doing, he halts and calls quickly over his shoulder, "Wait here." He scurries along the ground, his speed impressive, especially as he travels on only his two back legs. The thin wyvern body weaves between boulders and disappears into the circle of mist. The cries of the evildoers ring loudly a split second before sprays of dark blood burst into our small area, accompanied by the tearing of flesh.

Eir screws up her nose. "That's pretty gross."

"Yep." Britta shifts uncomfortably in her chair. "But needed."

The snakelike scales of Nidhogg weave in and out of the fog, his mouth open and his tongue licking the lingering blood off his maw. He appears more like a scavenger than a dragon, his fervor escalating after each attack and still shining in his dark eyes when he returns to our group. "That was a tasty meal. You lot are like a magnet for these creatures. Maybe I should have guests more often." Without waiting for a response, he falls into place and leads us away from the area.

After a while, we arrive at the banks of a river. Nidhogg's eyes are wide as he pauses on the bank, gazing at the water. "This is the river Gjoll." He lisps, "It's the barrier that surrounds Helheim. This is an added length to block the access from Niflheim to Helheim to stop the evildoers from crossing over. It's an added protection to Helheim." He waves his winged arms extravagantly. "The only way to cross is by the floating bridge."

The thudding of the horses' hooves approaches as Thor rounds Sleipnir back to the group after a brief sprint in the open-aired area. His bushy auburn eyebrows push together in a frown. "Why can't they cross it. Can't the evildoers swim?"

"Follow me." Nidhogg worms his way to the water. "Have a look."

The four dragons line up next to him on the bank, and they gaze into the water. Something silver flashes past too fast for them to focus on the object, yet all logical theories point to it being a fish. Another thing charges past quickly, not clear enough to rule out as a fish. When another object passes, a flash of silver catches my eye before it's carried away on the stream.

Elan moves to step into the water, then Nidhogg

dashes in front of us, blocking our way.

Britta chuckles and pulls up straight, towering above us on Tanda's strange midriff, shaped like a one-humped camel. "The river is full of fish."

Thor joins her laughter. "Then the dragons and Sleipnir can swim through that."

Nidhogg's eyes are wide. "Oh no. It's not fish that you see. Have a better look."

Hildr climbs off Drogon and treks to the edge before reaching for the water.

Nidhogg darts toward her. "Don't do that!"

She straightens and looks at him. "Why not?"

Nidhogg lowers his snout to her head height, his gaze moving from her face to the river. "Without touching it, stare down at the water and have a really good look."

Hildr studies the shallow water hard, her eyes flicking from one silver object to another. Slowly, she lowers her head to only a foot above the water. After staring at it for a moment longer, she blinks gradually and raises her wan face. "They're knives!" Her voice is barely audible as though speaking the words out loud will cause the weapons to chase her. "And they're traveling point-first through the water."

The wyvern nods earnestly. "That's right. Daggers and swords travel through these waters. Now you see why evildoers can't swim across."

Chapter Nine

F illed with disbelief, I pull my gaze from the water and to the wyvern. There is nothing written on his face or eyes to say that he's lying.

Hildr's battle-hardened face is ghostly white as she grabs her sword and slowly lowers the blade into the water. It only takes a moment before the muffled clanging of metal calls up to us as the emerged swords collide into the side of the blade. She plummets the steel deeper, and the clanging increases. The freckles on her face stand out as her skin turns impossibly paler. "They go farther down than just the top. Do these knives run all the way to the bottom?"

"They sure do," Nidhogg lisps then shrugs. "Well, for at least an awfully long way. Far enough that you can't swim underneath. Trust me. I've watched some evildoers try."

Then we can fly. Tanda's red eyes brighten with enthusiasm.

Thor slaps his thigh then points at Tanda. "Exactly! Surely the dragons can fly over the top. That was my plan."

Blank-faced, Nidhogg stares at her for a moment then says calmly, "You're a dragon. Use your dragon sight and have a look."

Tanda strains her long neck, raises her chin high, and scans the area above the river. Her scaly red eyebrows rise, and her red eyes flick in all directions above the surface of the water. "Wow! Knives and spears are even flying through the air." When she lowers her head to Nidhogg, her eyes are full of surprise.

Nidhogg's face is solemn. "Yes. They are farther than the average eye can see. It's proof, even though you have tough scales to protect your body, that they will slice through your membranous wings. Your rider would have very little chance of survival, with Thor having less of a chance trying to cross with his horse."

"That's just evil," Tanda says.

"Welcome to Niflheim." Nidhogg spreads his wings. "This is where evil people come and stay."

Thor fiddles with the reins of Sleipnir's saddle, his blue eyes filled with concern. "Then that blows my plan. I heard there were possibly knives in the water, but I thought the air was free and the dragons would be able to fly us across. How can we pass over?"

Nidhogg scans the water. "There is only one bridge that can be crossed."

"Where is it?" Thor asks.

Nidhogg hooks his tail in a half circle around his legs. "It hovers above the river, changing locations. Usually, when it faces Niflheim, there are only people getting offloaded onto the realm. I have never seen anyone taken off the realm. But you're the first lot of people who have visited, and you are alive. I have seen evildoers attempt to cross, but the giantess, Modgud, patrols the bridge. She must approve all souls before they can pass. It's the only way across this river."

Britta rubs her upper arm. "But won't the swords and spears flying through the air still pass through the bridge?"

The wyvern shakes his head. "No. Somehow, they divert their path and fly over or under the bridge, leaving the bridge free from all threats except for Modgud. It is the only safe passage. I hope Modgud will let you pass." Nidhogg starts to walk farther along the bank of the river. "Come. I'll lead you up the side of the bank until we find the bridge."

Trying to ignore the screams coming from the fog

inland, we stick close to Nidhogg's side, following him along the riverbank. Our gazes repetitively observe the streaks of silver as the swords flow with the strong current. Even the dragons look defeated against their threat. They might have flown over and received many bruises, but their wings wouldn't have withstood the constant penetration of their tender membranes, making it impossible to pass.

Each time the dragons peer across the river, their attention returns to us, with hopelessness filling their faces. As for the Valkyries, I had a slightly better chance to survive the crossing with my dragon-scale cloak, but I would not come out unscathed. Bruises would cover me, and the passing blades would slice any exposed skin. The others would have no chance without a dragon-scale coat.

We pass a rocky patch on the bank, and the dragons' talons click on the hard surface as we continue, trying to escape the cries in the distance. With Nidhogg escorting us, the evildoers seem to have lost interest in pursuing us. The word must spread rapidly around here.

With my eyes trained on the river, I keep a lookout for this bridge that Nidhogg has mentioned. Judging by the distance to the banks of Helheim, the bridge must be a considerable size, making it easier to spot. Yet with each step along the riverside, my hope of finding it diminishes.

We park on the side of the river to rest. In the never-ending darkness, it's impossible to tell how long we've been traveling. Hunger gnaws at my stomach, and after climbing off Elan's back, I reach into my bag and hand out some of the food that I'd gathered before the trip. I conjure some food for the dragons and a little more for us.

"Would you like a fresh cow or some other meat to take away the taste of decaying flesh?" I ask Nidhogg, determined to show our gratitude for his protection and guidance.

He sniffs the raw flesh of the cows that our dragons are eating and snorts to the side, expelling the smell from his nostrils. "I prefer my meat rotten, thank you."

The dragons and the riders screw up their noses in disgust, and Britta retches to the side. If it weren't for the extreme hunger groaning angrily in my stomach, constantly reminding me that I haven't eaten since this morning, I would be put off by my meal. I push away the image and let my hunger win the battle, devouring my food.

After finishing the last of her small meal, Britta curls up against Tanda's side. "Are we anywhere near there, where the bridge usually comes?"

Nidhogg watches the dragons finish the last of their carcasses, and his nose curls in clear disgust. "As I said, the bridge changes location. It swings from one to the other as Modgud patrols the borders of Helheim. The Gjoll river is large, and she has a lot of area to cover."

Eir brushes her fingers on her leather uniform. "How does Modgud test to see whether souls can cross her bridge?"

"Apparently, she asks questions from the soul," Nidhogg says.

"Surely they can't be that hard, can they?" Britta asks.

Nidhogg stops watching the dragons eat and shrugs. "I don't know. I've never tried to cross. Although, you may have a problem."

"Why's that?" Thor asks.

Nidhogg lies on one side. "You're not dead. She will be suspicious of you because you haven't passed. She only allows the dead through."

A deep rumble crawls up Drogon's throat. "I'll make her dead."

Nidhogg's rib cage rapidly rises and falls as he chuckles.

The brown dragon snorts and frowns at the wyvern. "What's so funny?"

"Wait until you see her." Nidhogg blows a raspberry then lisps. "I don't think that's going to be possible. But I'll let you decide." Ignoring Drogon's deadly glare, he asks, "Are you ready to keep moving, or would you like to stay here for a while?"

"Can we keep going, please?" A frown creases Eir's friendly face. "As enjoyable as it is to be around you, I would like to get out here."

Our guide jumps to his feet. "Okay, then let's keep going."

We reach patches of bank blocked by large boulders and circle them, leaving the bank momentarily. Each set of eyes takes turns scanning the river for a sign of a floating bridge. It has taken so long to spot it that we start to think it is a myth. When we finally see it in the distance, we breathe a sigh of relief. Tall golden arches frame the sides, glowing dully.

Nidhogg straightens. "Oh, goodie! Here comes the bridge, Gjallarbru."

Britta tucks a loose strand of hair behind her ear. "Is it made of gold?"

"Is that what all that shiny stuff is?" Nidhogg asks.

Britta gives him a bewildered look. "Yes."

"Then it's made of gold," the wyvern says cheerily.

The bridge sways from side to side, seemingly floating in midair.

Naga thinks it looks strange. What's it hanging from? The blue dragon's large eyes are concealed slightly by a frown.

Nidhogg waves a hand dismissively. "It hangs from one strand of hair."

"That's impossible." Tanda watches the wyvern with keen interest to see if he's lying. "That would snap."

Our host shrugs. "I haven't seen it snap yet. If you don't want to trust it, then you'll be stuck on Niflheim. It's up to you, but remember, it's your only way out."

We continue making our way along the edge of the river, closer to the approaching bridge. It awkwardly swings as it comes closer, taking with it my confidence that it will hold us.

It pauses when it reaches us, slowly swaying to a stop, with one opening facing us and the other stretching to Helheim. The platform rests at head height, making it hard for any of us to climb to its surface, yet we can see through it as though it is made from glass or crystal.

A figure with significant height slowly approaches from the middle of the bridge. It seems so frail in the distance, and with its painstakingly slow movements, I wonder whether the figure is dead. Inch by inch, it trudges over the bridge's surface until finally, the figure comes within our range of sight. I gasp.

Chapter Ten

Dry skin is vacuum-packed to the body so tightly that the giant appears to be a skeleton. Her cheeks are hollow and her eye sockets sunken, with even the bones on her feet standing out in the distance. Thin, wispy gray hair falls to her shoulders, and a worn-out off-white gown drapes over her frame. The footsteps thump lightly on the base of the transparent floored bridge as she makes slow progress to our end.

Watching her makes me wonder how she's considered a threat to anyone wanting to cross. It doesn't appear as though she would be able to move quickly enough to stop anyone.

As she approaches, I crane my neck to gaze at her face and spot the one strand of hair securing the bridge in the air. I wait for the bridge to tip in the direction of the weight, but it doesn't.

Britta whispers in my ear, "That's just wrong."

Her face is blank, and her skin is pale under the shine of the bridge.

"It would've been nice if Nidhogg had dropped us a hint of what to expect," I whisper. "I must admit, I wasn't prepared for this."

As the giant saunters closer, the sunken patches on her face seem to grow more profound, more ominous, and my skin crawls when the sunken eyes glower at us.

The ring of a sword sliding against its sheath shatters the silence. Hildr moves into a ready stance, her knees bent slightly, and her sword partially drawn. Even in the gloomy darkness, I can see her body is braced for a fight.

The giant stops several feet from the edge of the bridge, fixing us with her scowl. "Who dares to cross this bridge?"

I'm surprised the voice is loud and exploding with strength. It's not the sound I was expecting from this frail-looking creature. I gulp and, in the corner of my eye, catch one of us approaching the bridge.

Thor's shoulders straighten as he moves closer to the giantess. "It is I, Thor, god of thunder, who wishes to cross your bridge." He speaks with the air of the god that he is.

The giantess squats, lowering herself closer to Thor, yet her actions still convey superiority despite the decreased height. Wispy pieces of material flail around her thin body. They're thick enough to cover her gaunt flesh, yet I shiver when I think of the chilly air brushing against her skin.

"You're not dead. I can sense your alive soul. Only the dead shall pass into Helheim."

With arms crossed, Hildr flanks Thor. "Because we're alive, it's more reason that you should let us pass. You can't hold us here."

Modgud rises and scowls at the redheaded Valkyrie. "I will and do let pass all that I deem worthy. You cannot tell me what to do."

The ring of a drawn sword fills the air, and Hildr climbs swiftly onto Drogon's back, runs up his spine, and tiptoes along his neck, which is level with the bridge. She jumps over his horns and swings a sword at the giantess's stomach. "You will let us pass!"

My insides whirl. This isn't a peaceful solution. Thor has only begun to talk, yet Hildr has again jumped to a violent conclusion.

The giantess straightens to her full height, staring at Hildr. With a wave of her hand, an invisible force catches Hildr and knocks her off the bridge, back first and straight onto the ground at Drogon's feet. A massive *oomph* escapes her mouth, and she lies unmoving, winded and stunned.

Modgud crosses her arms across her bony chest,

feet splayed, ready, and glowers at us again. "I said, none shall pass unless I grant permission. You aren't dead, and you cannot pass."

Thor inclines his head respectfully. "Please forgive my comrade for the way she acted. She is a Valkyrie, one with a short temper and primed for war. She means you no harm."

Modgud flails an arm in Hildr's direction. "It does not appear that way. When one runs at me with a sword, it isn't an act of peace."

Thor's loud breath hisses out of his nose. "No. I have to agree. But we cannot find another way out of here. We ended up in the realm by accident. We were supposed to go to Helheim first."

When Modgud doesn't respond, he continues, "We are in search of my brother Balder. He has died a dishonorable death, and we wish to speak to Hel over this." He clasps his hands in front of him in a plea. "I beg of you to please reconsider and let myself and each of us cross with our companions that we may pursue this."

The lack of empathy in the giantess's eyes has me biting my tongue.

The guardian raises her chin. "The realm of Niflheim is only for evildoers. The despicable crimes they have committed, including murder and rape, are unforgivable. I do not take people from this area." She turns to leave.

Thor holds up a hand in a silent gesture to stop. "I promise you, we're none of those. But we have entered through the world tree and cannot return." He pleads with open arms. "Balder, my brother, isn't here. We have searched and discussed it with Nidhogg." He turns to our escort.

The wyvern nods enthusiastically. "Yes. What he says is true. I saved them from the evildoers. They shouldn't be here. They'll taste disgusting."

I cast him a side glance and notice the others doing the same.

I return my gaze to Modgud and catch an amused expression on her face. "Aren't they dead enough for you, Nidhogg?"

Although I wonder whether she is joking, her voice remains intense.

Groaning, Hildr slowly pushes herself off the ground and into a standing position.

Modgud watches her keenly. "Does this one rise to rechallenge me?"

Hildr inclines her head slightly. "I do not wish to challenge you again. I apologize. I acted in haste. I was upset you seemed unmoving and not willing to let us through."

Modgud raises her chin. "I have not decided yet."

Britta moves next to me. "And what will help you decide?"

The goddess moves an arm horizontally, indicating the whole group. "Each of you must state your reason for crossing."

"But we are all here for the same reason," Thor protests. "Why can't you take my word for it?"

A glimmer of annoyance passes through her sunken eyes, and Thor cringes. "Each of you has a different soul. You must individually pass my regulations before I let you pass." She plants a threatening scowl on Hildr. "That's including you."

Following a disturbing chuckle, Thor says, "I understand that you have rules to live by, but we cannot leave anybody behind."

Modgud's face hardens. "That, again, is up to you. I will still pass you all individually or not pass you. Take it or leave it."

Worry courses through me as I gaze over the river, watching as the silver flashes of swords pass through and imagining them arching over the bridge.

Nidhogg slithers next to me, and I cringe at his words. "There is no other way. You have to do as she says or stay on Niflheim."

"Does that include the dragons?" Britta asks.

Modgud eyes the dragons individually. "That is the rule for anything that has a soul."

Chapter Eleven

"Yes, but..." Britta protests.

Tanda nudges her from behind. *Don't ask for trouble. We must all do this. There is no way around it. You Valkyries, Thor, and Zildryss go first. The dragons have more of a chance to cross unaided.*

Britta gazes deep into Tanda's red eyes, her forehead wrinkling as if concerned. "But we don't want to leave anybody behind."

Tanda levels her gaze on all the people. *This is what has to be done. You cannot stay here.*

Naga's blue eyes are wide and earnest. *She is right. You must go. Although Nidhogg has looked after us, this is not the place for us. We must all go through her assessment. If the dragons don't make it, we will deal with it.*

Eir strokes the top of Naga's head, and he closes his eyes briefly before giving her an affectionate gaze.

"I will go first." Thor moves closer to the bridge. "I'll stand guard at the other end, waiting for you all to come." He stands tall, fiddling with the handle of his hammer, and expands his chest. "As I have stated, I am Thor, god of the thunder, and son of Odin. I come in search of my brother, Balder. Once I have completed my mission, I shall leave this land and return to Asgard."

Modgud moves to the edge of the bridge, squats, and towers over the large god, scrutinizing his every feature. "If you think that I am a tough ruler, then wait until you meet Hel. I don't like your chances. Still, it's your fight with the goddess." She returns to a stand before drawing a long staff like a sword off her back. "You may pass, Thor, god of thunder."

Nidhogg claps his front talons. "Yay for you, Thor."

The giantess taps the staff on the bridge. Suddenly, Thor projects and lands next to her, his face shaken over the unexpected transport. It takes him a moment to adjust. Then he gazes down through the transparent surface before slowly pacing away, cautiously treading his big boots, his eyes fixed on the single hair as though waiting for it to snap. It's evident that he fears the bridge will tilt him off or collapse into the water from the additional weight.

Somehow, the hair remains intact, and the bridge maintains its balance.

"State your name and business." Modgud's powerful voice pulls my attention away from Thor.

"I am Eir, a Valkyrie from Asgard. I also come in search of Balder and promise, to leave the moment our business is done."

Modgud whacks the staff against the bottom of the bridge, instantly transporting Eir from the ground to her side.

"Thank you," she whispers. Obviously dazed and confused, Eir tentatively follows Thor over the bridge.

Nidhogg applauds loudly.

Britta stands below the entrance to the bridge. Her long dark hair falls down her back in a ponytail, and her shoulders are straight. "I am Britta, Valkyrie of Asgard, and I come in search of Balder, the well-liked light god with a peaceful heart. I promise to leave the moment my business is done."

Modgud straightens and scrutinizes Britta, observing every feature. Her wait is longer than the ones for Thor and Eir, and I start to pick at my nails. Modgud squints then whacks her staff on the bridge. Instantly, the Valkyrie is transported to stand next to the giantess. Her eyes are wide with apprehension and uncertainty as she searches for the reason the bridge hasn't broken from its bond. With tentative light footsteps, she follows Eir across the bridge.

The wyvern dances on the bank not far from the group. "Look at you lot go!"

Zildryss's talons scratch my shoulders, and I twist my neck to peer at him. "It's your turn, little guy."

Without wasting a second, he pushes off and flies in front of Modgud, trying to land on her shoulders. The giantess swings her staff at him in an attempt to ward him off.

I raise my hand as though to protect him before realizing its uselessness. "Stop! Please. He can only communicate by touch. I promise he won't hurt you."

Modgud's sunken eyes are uncertain as she assesses my sincerity, still not allowing him to land on her. "Is he a long-mouthed guardian?"

"Yes. He's a special little dragon, but he doesn't speak. The most you'll get is a couple of squeaks."

Modgud stretches out her bony arm, covered in dehydrated skin. "Then you may land on me, young dragon."

Gleefully, Zildryss flips in the air and lands softly on her outstretched arm, dropping his belly against her skin. The giantess's face turns blank, and a look of knowledge passes through her eyes just before she announces, "You may pass, young Zildryss."

Nidhogg claps lightly. "Yay, little guy."

Looking quite pleased with himself, Zildryss faces Nidhogg with almost a smile on his face as he licks alternating eyes then quickly follows the two Valkyries.

Modgud's sunken eyes land on me, and after a moment of panic, I straighten my shoulders and make my request. "Please let the horse and dragons go first."

The giantess nods, and after a whinny, Sleipnir passes over. Elan insists Naga goes first, then Tanda, with Nidhogg cheering each successful pass, leaving Drogon, Hildr, Elan, and myself.

The sunken eyes land on me again. I swallow, attempting to move the lump stuck in my throat, then announce who I am. A quick tap of the staff has me standing next to the giant, trying to recover from the different transportation and a magic that wasn't my own. Nidhogg's cheerful clapping sends shock waves through my head. It's a strange feeling, walking on a transparent surface, and it takes some getting used to.

By the time I reach halfway, I'm stopped by the distressed protests of Hildr back on shore. "What? That's not fair!"

I glance over my shoulder. Nidhogg clasps his front talons together, his face serious.

"No. I don't believe I will let you pass." Modgud's voice is firm and unforgiving. She raises her chin and calls, "Next!"

"Wait! Please!" Hildr calls. She runs a hand through her spiky red hair, her feet shuffling nervously. "I apologize for my haste in attacking you before. I was purely in a battle mind. It was nothing personal. I've been known to be quite hasty to fight. This was just one of those cases." She smiles sweetly.

I clamp my teeth, waiting for Modgud's response.

"Then you shall think before you leap next time. If you have a next time." There's no forgiveness in her voice. "Next!" the guardian of the bridge calls.

Before I can set foot in Hildr's direction to see if I can help, Drogon stands protectively beside her. *Please, let her go.* Although his words are respectful, they sound like they have been said through gritted teeth, and a warning lies in his eyes. *She has been known to have a bad temper and often acts before she thinks, much like myself.*

Elan moves in front of Drogon as though blocking him from instigating an attack. Her broad golden body dwarfs his larger size. *That's true. These two have always been short-tempered, but they mean well. Please reconsider.*

Modgud doesn't hesitate. "I do not have to, and I will not."

Chapter Twelve

Elan blocks Drogon from the gatekeeper as his feet shuffle aggressively. Hildr's posture changes as belligerence takes hold. Her hand moves to her sword hilt, and I know I have to stop her before she does something else stupid. I break into a sprint, calling out, "Wait!"

Hildr's hand pauses over the hilt, and at the same time, Modgud turns and watches me approach. With each step, the giantess seems to grow more intimidating.

A coldness passes through the guardian's eyes. "What do you want? I have let you through. You shall pass to the end, or there will be consequences."

Hesitant and unsure, I take a couple of more paces. I'm not going to let my insecurity stop me from helping my friend. No one is going to be left behind. Eyeing the giant warily, I raise my palms, facing them toward her. "I understand. But there must be some way or a bargain that we can make with you in order to let them through." When she looks unmoving, I blurt, "There must be some way around your rules."

Modgud tosses her staff from one palm to the other, her eyes distant. I feel a lump growing in my throat as her eyes turn cold. Her dry lips curl up at the edges in an evil smirk. When she refocuses on me, I almost choke on the lump. There is definitely a sinister amusement there. "There is one thing."

Nidhogg sucks in a breath. "Oh no. Not the thing!"

My heart leaps with both hope and apprehension. "What is it?" I dare to step a tiny bit forward.

"If you wish for your friend to be able to cross the bridge, then you must part with a piece of your soul as a promise that you will make sure she does as she is told and behaves in Helheim."

"And what will that mean for me?" My voice cracks.

The guardian's sneer grows. "That will mean that if you die while I possess it, you will be tied to Niflheim, even if you die a warrior."

My cheeks turn clammy, and my jaw drops.

"You're not doing that, Kara." Hildr threatens me with a glare. "I'll work something out. It's my rash actions that got me here in the first place. I should bear the consequences."

I ignore her demands and steel my emotions, focusing on the giantess. "Will you return that piece to me when we leave Helheim?"

Modgud tosses her staff from hand to hand. The action looks strange without evidence of any muscles in her hands. It takes all my effort not to scream for her to hurry up and make a decision and stop leaving us in the lurch. Eventually, her hands still. "If you promise to keep her contained and make sure she behaves. If you manage this, I will give you back your soul when I escort you on the other side back to Yggdrasil and the fiery Valkyrie has left Helheim."

"Don't you dare, Kara!" Hildr cries, pulling at her short red hair. "I cannot let that sit on my conscience."

"And I can't leave you behind." I stare into the deep dark eyes of Modgud, struggling to swallow the lump in my throat. "Okay. I'll do it."

It was hard to get those simple words past the giant lump in my throat. It wouldn't budge. Still, it brought me some peace to know that I wasn't leaving a friend behind, and all will work out in the end if Modgud keeps her promise.

The giantess moves toward me, reaching out to touch me with too much eagerness. I stumble back a few steps. "First, I need you to let Hildr go past before I give you a piece of my soul."

Annoyance flashes over the giantess's face. "If I do this, then you must remain within my reach until the trade is complete."

"No, Kara!" Hildr's freckles push together as her face distorts. "You can't do this."

The gravity of my actions weighs on my shoulders as I stare into her eyes. "It's done. The deal is made."

Before Hildr can protest again, Modgud taps her staff on the bridge, instantly transporting Hildr next to her. The Valkyrie stares at the guardian with eyes full of threats and distaste but thankfully refrains from striking the goddess. Hildr says, "You better stick to your promise. I will stick to my promise as long as you stick to yours. You must return the piece of her soul when we leave the realm." Still staring the goddess down, she slowly backs down the bridge and toward the others who have passed.

My insides tear as I watch her go. My only comfort is in knowing that I haven't left her behind. My feet are rooted to the spot, and suspicion rises that it's not just my terror holding me there but also magic. I test my feet and find that it is true. Modgud has secured me to the spot, disabling me to leave until she has retained what I promised.

Gnawing catches my attention, and I spot Nidhogg chewing his talons, his face twisted with trepidation.

Long spindly fingers reach for me, and I cringe when her dried, hard flesh touches mine. She looks so frail. Her skin is so thin and dry, her hair almost transparent and her sunken eyes eerie. Yet when her hands close around my wrist, I suck in a gasp. The weak-looking skeleton is strong, deceptively more robust than she looks. She tucks her staff on her back and reaches for my chest. Instantly, I feel my life force drained from me. I cry out, feeling my soul torn and a piece removed. Judging by the pain, it feels like a lot more than just a small piece.

Elan stomps her feet on the ground, leaving talon marks on the bank. *That's enough. Surely you have your piece of soul, if not more than what you should be taking.*

The giantess's hand remains, draining parts of my soul as she observes my golden dragon with amusement. Nidhogg cowers behind Elan, his eyes wide with dejection and indecision.

Drogon stands to attention at Elan's side. *She's right. You should have your piece. Her debt for the agreement is paid.*

Gasps of terror seep from me as Modgud slowly pulls her hand away from my chest, ripping with it the detached piece of soul. I stagger backward and suck in a breath. It feels as though a carriage has run over me. It takes a few moments for me to regain enough strength to move my feet.

Between her fingers, the giantess grasps something shiny, and horror fills me as she tucks it into a pocket of her flimsy gown and zips it. With a look of triumph, she pats the pocket lightly as though just retrieving a prized possession. "It will remain here until you have kept your word."

At first, I'm too shocked to move let alone say anything. My ears ring in distress, barely processing that the giantess has retrieved her staff from her back again before using the point to nudge me along the bridge toward the middle. Slowly placing one foot in front of the other, I trudge forward, aiming for Helheim. The lingering shock causes the pressure in my ears to change, and I work my jaw to pop them.

As though oblivious to what she's done, Modgud paces to the edge of the bridge and calls, "Next!"

Elan indicates to Drogon, pushing him forward slightly. *You go next.*

Concern fills Drogon's eyes. *Are you sure, Elan? You should go first. You're more important than me.* His brown eyes are serious and beaming with respect. *You're the next leader of the dragons in the wasteland. You should be protected.*

And what sort of leader would I be if I let my dragons die? she asks. *No. That can't happen. You can go first.*

When Drogon balks at the idea, Elan uses her authoritative voice. *Go, Drogon! I insist.*

Commanded to go forward, Drogon tentatively moves in front of Elan and gazes expectantly at Modgud. *I am Drogon from Asgard's wastelands. I, too, have come to help find Balder.*

I pause about a quarter way along the bridge and watch Drogon's progression, hoping for the best yet fearing the worst. A look at Nidhogg's cowering face peeking from behind Elan doesn't bring me the confidence I need.

A dark cloud seems to surround Modgud, as though sensing something dark and ominous, and her body stiffens. "You are the dragon that is bonded with that redheaded rider. The one that only barely got through."

Wariness passes over Drogon's dark features, yet he doesn't answer.

"You must stay behind."

What? Drogon splutters.

The giantess tugs at a fraying piece of gown. "I won't let you pass."

Chapter Thirteen

My face is completely numb, and my heart drops to my feet. I'm still struggling to pull it together after the giantess took a piece of my soul. If that's what she wants for Drogon to be able to pass... my knees turn weak at the thought.

Elan stands, bracing on all fours beside the brown dragon. *What? You can't do that.*

"She can, and she will." Nidhogg moves out from behind her. His uneasiness remains.

Elan protests, *But Drogon isn't dead.*

"Yeah, I get it. But she's done a lot of refusing before, just not to alive beings." The wyvern slithers next to Drogon. "If it helps, I'll be glad for your company. We can chew the roots of Yggdrasil and eat the evildoers together."

Drogon's lip curls in disgust. "Ah. Thanks, but no thanks, Nidhogg."

Elan ignores the exchange and continues her

protest. *But he's done nothing wrong, other than being associated with Hildr.*

The gatekeeper straightens, her face set in a show of determination.

It takes all my willpower to push my legs to move, back to the dragons and the gatekeeper. "What do you require for Drogon to pass?" My words are barely a mutter, yet I'm determined that my weakness won't affect his outcome. "There must be some way for him to pass as well."

Modgud looks quite pleased with herself as she dusts her worn gown and steeples her fingers, tapping them against each other repetitively. She eyes me with a sick curiosity. "I could easily do another deal like before, yet observing you, I don't believe you could handle it."

Her grin makes me want to cower.

"And to think I only took a small piece of your soul. Are you willing to go through that again?"

My knees buckle, and I stagger to the edge of the bridge, grabbing hold of its golden side. Just the thought of going through it again is almost too much to bear, let alone actually doing it again. Breathing deeply, I focus on the ground, willing myself to be strong and convincing myself that I can do this. The tiny bit of strength I gather allows me to straighten my spine and slowly raise my eyes to Modgud, facing the evil intent lying in the goddess's eyes. I open my mouth to speak, hoping that the right words come out when Elan's voice cuts through our thoughts.

There's no way she's going to part with another bit of her soul. Take a piece of mine.

"No!" The harsh croaky voice doesn't sound like mine. I lick my parched lips and focus on Elan.

Drogon's voice cuts through my attempts to stare off my dragon. *There's no way I'm letting you lose a piece of yourself for me.* He stands in front of Elan protectively, trying to block her from Modgud's reach. *It's just not happening. Whether you're in charge of the dragons or not.*

Elan straightens, towering over the brown dragon despite the additional height his horns give him, and unwavering, glares at him. *Exactly what you said, Drogon. I am in charge of you, and I'm the next in line to rule over the dragons. You must do as I command.*

It's so rare to see Elan take control and use her authority that the shock gives me relief. In the same instance, she is taking charge, and she's willing to give up part of herself for her dragons. I wish I could do it for her, but I don't think I can go through it again.

Despite being put in his place, Drogon continues to stand protectively in front of Elan. His excessively horned body standing ridged and defensive, he's determined to protect his leader. When Elan tries to move past him, he bares his teeth in a snarl. *I do not wish to harm you, Elan, my respected leader. But I won't stand by and watch the gatekeeper take a piece of your soul. I don't want you to give up part of yourself so that I may cross the bridge into Helheim.*

Elan snaps her teeth threateningly at Drogon. *It's not your wish that I'm concerned about. You are part of my army, and I'm not leaving a soldier down. Now cross the bridge. That's an order! Then I can get this lousy exchange over and done with.*

Greed washes over Modgud's face. "I've never had a dragon's soul before."

Malice crawls under Drogon's skin. *A piece of a dragon's soul.*

Modgud raises her chin, staring down her nose at him. *Yes. A piece, to be precise. But still, I have never had a portion of a dragon's soul before. I will make the exchange.* She taps her staff on the bridge, and Drogon transports to her side, teeth snarling, and horns lowered at the gatekeeper. To honor their agreement, he doesn't attack her, but the threat was there.

The brown dragon wraps a wing around me and nudges me along the bridge. *Come on, Kara. I don't like it any more than you do, but we have to go. Elan won't want you to watch this. It nearly killed her watching you lose a piece of yours.*

My feet move like chunks of lead, plodding reluctantly along the clear bridge floor. "I don't want to go. I don't want to leave Elan to face that alone. I want to be with her when it happens."

Elan told me she doesn't want you to watch. She doesn't want you to feel any more pain. You have been through enough. He nudges me forward with his nose to move me along faster, purposely missing me with his horns. *Now come along. She will follow close behind.*

Slowly, my feet clunk one in front of the other as I'm pushed gently forward by Drogon. Through my distressed, dazed vision, I see the others waiting on the shore on the other side. Swords whoosh above me. The sound seems louder, as though trying to block out any protests from Elan. This isn't right. I should be by her side.

As much as it would hurt me to see it, I want to turn back and be with her and help her take the pain. I should be there to insert my magic into her, to help calm her afterward.

Twisting, I attempt to turn around, but Drogon blocks my attempts and nudges me forward, angling me with any limb he can spare, even his wings, narrowly missing me with the hook on the tip of the fold.

We are mostly across the bridge when pain shoots down my bond with Elan. She must have accidentally let that one through. Adrenaline courses through me, and I weave my way past Drogon's defenses in time to see Elan buckle to her knees.

"Elan!" I scream.

Nidhogg watches from the ground in a frozen stupor, Elan lying at Modgud's feet. A strange flash surrounds the golden dragon.

Tears stream down my face, and my exhausted legs attempt to move in her direction. I'm still too weak from my own experience, leaving me hopeless to fight against Drogon's resistance. Modgud's hand rests on Elan's broad chest, and her body heaves as the gatekeeper drags a piece of her soul from her.

My legs give, and Drogon gathers me in his wings.

Thor's deep voice calls from the bank. "Kara. You must come." His arms are spread, reaching for me.

Through eyes blurred by grief and tears, I spot the other friends on the bank calling to me, urging me forward. "I need to go back." Huskiness taints my voice as I try to convince Drogon. "I need to help her."

You can't. She's on her own in this. Drogon's mind-speak voice cracks with emotion. *Hopefully, Modgud will keep her bargain and let her cross the bridge.*

Chapter Fourteen

"Let me go back. I need to go back!" I cry, reaching out as though I can touch her even though she's across the bridge.

We had left it and were standing on the bank. I attempt to climb back onto the bridge, yet my feet don't want to move. It feels as though claws are grasping my ankles and stopping me.

"Take me back. We need to help her cross." As the words exit my mouth, I know how stupid they sound. As if I can help an enormous dragon like Elan cross a long bridge. I can hardly move myself.

Strong, muscular arms wrap around me and pull me close against their chest. Instantly, I know it's Thor wrapping me in a bear hug, trying to comfort me. "We'll work it out, Kara. Just relax. Elan is a big strong dragon."

Naga sits beside me and places his snout on my leg. His warmth seeps through my leather uniform, and his presence helps calm my panicking heart. *You survived having a piece of your soul removed. Elan will too.*

Resting my hand on his snout, I gaze at Elan's crumpled form. She looks damaged, and it's hard to drum up hope that she will be all right. If my strong dragon and leader of the dragons looks that damaged after losing a piece of her soul, I must have looked terrible, probably even dead.

Eir gently caresses my cheek. "Relax, Kara. You look as pale as one of these dead people. We'll work it out." She brushes my hair behind my shoulder. "Hold still. I'll inject some healing energy into you."

Warmth flows into me when she touches my neck. It flows up into my face and brain and down into my body. Having the physical part healed brings a sensation of peace to my soul, although I know healing isn't possible. A strange calming sensation washes over me, softening my anguish, and I stop fighting, relaxing my back against Thor's chest. My eyes remain trained on Elan.

It's surprising that the bridge doesn't tilt to one side from the weight of a heavy dragon. It should have been more than enough to send it out of balance. Under the gatekeeper's amused gaze, Elan attempts to climb to her feet. Her legs splay as she attempts to push herself up. It takes a few tries, but she eventually rises to all fours and slowly places one foot in front of the other. Elan slips after several steps and starts the whole process again, and I grasp Naga's talon and squeeze it. Her pace is exceedingly slow, and it tears my heart that she is doing this alone.

When she reaches the middle, she slips again and lands on her chest, her jaw slamming onto the transparent bridge platform. Slowly, she pushes up and continues along the bridge, each step increasing in pace. The dragons start to cheer her on, and her efforts strengthen and improve before us.

Movement at the end of the bridge catches my eye, and my muscles tense again when Modgud slowly walks behind Elan. I worry that the giantess is about to do something else terrible to my friend, then she stops at the halfway mark. "Hurry up, dragon. I need to move."

Despite her struggles, Elan manages to scowl over her shoulder at the keeper of the bridge. Her pace continues to quicken from the encouragement of the group on shore. When she reaches the edge, a loud cheer erupts, growing louder as she jumps onto the bank. The dragons dance around her, nudging her playfully, and even though she still looks exhausted, the worry visibly lifts. Scrambling to my feet, I weave through the rowdy dragons and wrap my arms around her leg.

Eir slips a hand under Elan's scale, injecting healing light into her soft skin underneath.

"Thank you, Eir," I say, grateful that my friend is adept in healing and is unafraid to use it even though her healing of me only moments before would have drained some of her energy.

Without taking her eyes off Elan, she says, "You don't have to thank me. It's my pleasure. I would do it in a heartbeat, and you know it."

"I know. But I still think you should know I appreciate it," I say. "I don't think I could drum up the energy right now."

"I know." She smiles softly. A strand of brown hair falls over her face, and she blows it away from her eyes, her hands still inserted under Elan's scales.

The corner of my eye catches some movement, and I turn to see the bridge, Gjallarbru, swinging up the river, the glow from the gold lighting up different sections of the water. Modgud stands in the middle, her legs splayed and staff in hand. Momentarily, the bridge swings wildly with the initial start-up, the rocking slowing as it progresses farther up the river. The flying swords and spears arch over the bridge as though repelled by an opposing magnetic force.

With the glow of the bridge gone, we can no

longer see Nidhogg across the other side of the Gjoll river.

"That giantess is one being I'm not upset to see the last of." Thor shifts next to Elan and places a hand on her nose. "What happened over there?"

My ribs heave, remembering the nightmare that played out. "Modgud took a piece of my soul so Hildr could cross, then she took a piece of Elan's so Drogon could cross." Exhaustion racks my body, even just talking about it.

"That's terrible." Thor stomps his foot. "Absolutely atrocious. Are you going to get it back?"

"That was her promise." I look at the dark, starless sky and close my eyes. "Whether she honors that promise when we leave is yet to be seen."

"Are you all right?" Thor places a hand on my shoulder.

"I'm weak, and it feels like something is missing. I should strengthen as time goes on." I have no idea if that is true, but I try to remain positive for my friends' sake. "Hopefully, the gatekeeper keeps her promises." I gaze at Elan. "She did promise to return your piece of soul, too, didn't she?"

Looking slightly more alert, Elan huffs. *I guess you can call it an agreement. Like you said, as to whether she sticks to it, I am not sure.*

Thor runs a hand over her snout. "If she doesn't,

we will find a way. I can't have my favorite eating companion with a disadvantage."

When Elan doesn't bite back with a retort, he casts her a concerned look. "Are you both okay to continue? If you aren't, just say so, and we'll wait."

Concentrating on my body, I assess all the aches and test how it feels. "I believe I am, but Elan may not be. It took me a while to get over it."

Don't be ridiculous. Elan stretches, letting a grimace escape before plastering on a strong face. *I'll be fine in just a moment.* She grins, showing off her extensive array of sharp teeth in her usual cheeky fashion, and it gives me hope. She may be putting on a brave face, but her cheekiness lurks, which is a good sign.

"So, are you taking it slow, then?" I ask her.

Whatever gave you that idea? She broadens her smile until it looks almost painful. *But yes, that would be good.* She drops her smile.

We turn away from the river and gaze up at Helheim. The thick mist is gone, yet a deep chill wraps us. I rub my arms vigorously, trying to warm them. I'm grateful that Nidhogg had a pond for us to wash in and where we could change into clean clothes. The new uniform is slightly damp from our extended time in the mist. It retains most of the warmth but not enough. I huddle close to Elan, soaking in her heat.

A small light cuts through the darkness, accentuating the peaks of the enormous mountain range before us. My heart skips a beat at the thought of having to climb it, and relief floods through me when I spot the small gap between the range, almost purposefully hidden behind a mountain.

Thor points in the direction of the opening. "Now, there's a welcome sight."

Our joy is short-lived as glowing red eyes emerge from around the other side of the mountains.

Chapter Fifteen

The glowing red eyes stalk closer, growing larger and seemingly taller with each step. It's impossible to make out the creature they belong to with the dark mountains blocking its outline from the uncanny dull light shining in the distance.

Behind us, the whistling of flying swords and spears reminds us that the running river is more ominous than it appears and there is no place to retreat. We are stuck, blocked by the Gjoll river, especially now that the bridge has moved on.

Slowly, the glowing red eyes approach down the hill, accentuating the creature's huge size. It's much bigger than us, and although the dragons are taller, it could still pose a threat. We move to the side, the shift causing the pass to open, shining the dull light and outlining the creature. The soft rattle of chains being dragged across a rock's surface gives me hope that the animal is restrained, and we are out of its reach, although it is impossible to tell in the darkness, and every muscle in my body seizes with tension, waiting for it to pounce.

Britta freezes. "Oh, Vanir! It's like Fenrir but on steroids."

The muscles in the hound's legs bulge, and as it steps away from the cover of the mountain, its face is revealed. A giant maw of exposed teeth snarls at us. I'd have to agree with Britta. The hound is like a larger Fenrir in his aggressive state. We move to the side, and it imitates us, exposing the end of its chain. It isn't connected. The chain is broken, and the hound is free. My heart thumps rapidly against my ribs as though demanding to be released.

"Great! Just exactly what we need. We just got through one bad spot." Hildr grasps her sword hilt, and metal squeals.

Britta swirls her hands, a movement indicating that she is drawing on her magic.

Eir stands between the two Valkyries and presses her palm on top of Hildr's sword hand, stopping the draw, and gently grabs Britta's wrist. "No. There are better ways to solve this." Her peace-filled voice is barely audible.

"Do you really think the peaceful approach is going to work in Helheim?" Hildr says through gritted teeth.

Britta shakes off Eir's grasp yet holds back from gathering more magic.

"It can't hurt to try. The aggressive way certainly didn't work with Modgud." Eir gestures to me then Elan, whose shoulders are still slumped slightly. "Look what happened to Kara and Elan. They paid for their aggressiveness. Maybe there is a peaceful way around the hound, one that will help us pass without anyone getting hurt."

Slowly, Eir progresses, her boots crunching on gravel, and stones scatter to the side. She bypasses Thor, and when she nears the beast, she calls out, "Greetings, my friend. We come in peace. We merely wish to travel through Helheim to visit Hel. Will you please grant us access?"

A low grumble sounds from ahead, the sound crescendoing until it reaches a deep, throaty growl. "What? Do you think that I'm going to let you pass simply because you ask nicely?"

It takes a moment for the shock to pass. The hound can talk, just like Fenrir does.

"There is only one way to pass me," the hound snarls.

"And what is that, may I ask?" Eir assumes her sweetest voice. "Perhaps we can comply."

"You must supply me with Helcake." He bares his teeth. "Have you not read the legends?"

"I'm sorry, I didn't have a chance to read the legends of Helheim before I came. What does this Helcake look like, and where can I get it?"

I can tell Eir is fishing for a description to see if one of us can conjure it with our magic, but the hound just sneers.

"If you haven't read the legends of Garm, the famous hound of Helheim, then that is information for me to know and you to find out." The hound leers, still blocking the entrance to the mountains.

Eir's shoulders cave slightly as though her hope has been smashed. Her despair doesn't last for long, and strength returns to her limbs. "Give us a little while, and we will supply the cake."

The hound growls, moving his paws from side to side, and a chain clinks with the movement before he stands guard, ready to attack. His glowing red eyes constrict. "You can't conjure the cake by magic. In truth, the cake comes only to those who would give to the needy. Only your soul can supply you with the cake. And if you don't deserve it, you can't pass." He lowers, his form clearly ready to pounce.

Instead of focusing on the threat before her, Eir stills with her hands held out, and I imagine her eyes are closed. The moments tick on forever, as we are too scared to breathe heavily in case we break her concentration. After a while, something appears in her palm, and she holds it up to the hound. "Is this the Helcake you wish for?"

The hound sniffs the open air, and even though he's still some distance away, his sense of smell seems to be stronger than that of a normal hound. The chain rattles some more as he slowly shifts closer. "It appears to be." The hound sounds surprised. "You must have a pure and giving heart." The aggressiveness melts from his form as he approaches Eir, continually sniffing. "Yes. This is it."

Eir places the cake on a large rock nearby.

He devours it, his tongue lavishly licking his maw. "You have instant access into Helheim."

Eir places a palm over her heart and chuckles. "I'm honored that I have been granted this." She moves daringly close to the hound, setting my nerves on edge. "May I ask what your name is?"

The hound straightens. "Oh, I thought I told you. My name is Garm. I'm the protector of Helheim's entrance. This is not my usual place, but I sensed someone crossing the barrier into Helheim, and I broke free to make sure the intruders are worthy."

Eir waves a hand dismissively. "We're not intruders. We're just visitors. I'm pleased to meet you." She casts a knowing look at Hildr, rubbing in the fact that the peaceful way won, before turning back to Garm. "May my friends also pass?"

Garm's posture stiffens again, and his glowing red eyes hold a new wariness. "They must also provide me with the Helcake. Each of them must have given to the needy in some way. Whatever their outcome, you may pass." He stands aside, and Eir passes Garm and waits closer to the mountain range as Naga approaches.

The Helcake wastes no time landing in front of Naga, and the peaceful blue dragon straightens his back, looking pleased with himself. *Look. Naga is happy. Naga managed to get the cake.* His tone is joyful.

Garm steps aside and lets him through. Sleipnir is next, then Thor, Britta, Tanda, Elan, and me. Each of us quickly receives a piece of Helcake. The wait for Drogon's and Hildr's cake is a little slower but eventually arrives. The last to come through is Zildryss, the Helcake appearing before the little dragon moves close to the hound.

When we're all on the side of Helheim, we face Garm and bow in unison, thanking him for our access before traveling through the gap between the mountains. As we peak the crest, we stare at the valley below. The land is scattered with many souls. I expect to see their heads down like they are studying the ground and in desperate hopelessness. Instead, these souls seem strangely joyous, displaying a mix of elves, dragons, giants, and all the creatures from the realms attached to Yggdrasil. Somehow, despite their differences while alive, they all seem peaceful and unthreatened.

Hildr clears her voice and casts Thor a side glance. "I know it's not what you want to hear, but if we don't get Balder out, this may not be such a bad place. Everyone seems content here."

Thor's forehead pushes together into a deep frown, his red eyebrows crowning his eyes like a thunderstorm. "If I don't return with Balder, Frigg will skin me alive. She will never forgive me. Not to mention the punishment I'll receive from my father because I've disappointed him and failed his wife."

Chapter Sixteen

Tentatively, we peak the crest then enter the valley, weaving our way along the path, avoiding any of the souls wandering through Helheim. Despite the place not being grief-stricken and soul-tormenting like Niflheim, there is a strangeness about how everyone is acting.

Thor's bushy eyebrows continue to bunch over his eyes like a confused cloud. "I know you said that this isn't such a bad ending, Hildr, but I can't see any god or warrior enjoying this. There seems to be no purpose to their lives. Although not tormented, they seem to be aimlessly wandering as though they don't have a routine or purpose. I can't see anyone who is striving for an afterlife in Valhalla enjoying this. After a while, I think this aimlessness would send them crazy." He indicates different sections around us as far as we can see. "After all, what is there to do?" He shrugs, a hopeless expression taking over his face as though the madness of being here is already haunting him.

Hildr tugs at the tips of her short hair. "Good point. I believe this would drive both Drogon and me mad. There is nothing to do, and there seem to be no challenges available, just pointless wandering."

Meandering through the hillsides, we stumble across a path and follow it through the aimless souls, hoping it leads us toward Hel and where she is stationed. The trail leads up into the shadows of the mountains. The souls dissipate as we move into the deeper shadow. A river rests under a cave cloaked with the darkness of the mountain. When we pass the cave entrance, several hisses echo against its walls, and we jump back.

"What's that?" Britta clings to Tanda's far side.

Tanda's brilliant red eyes glow with wariness. *The cave is filled with numerous venomous snakes. Whatever you do, don't enter the river. The snakes seem to be using it as their swimming hole.*

Thor scratches his bushy beard. "Oh, I've heard of this one. These snakes breed here and travel downstream to Niflheim to torment the evildoers with their venom."

Britta's nose screws with obvious disgust. "Eww!"

Our footsteps quicken as we leave the dreaded

cave area. When we weave through the mountain ranges, the darkness grows less intense and pulls my mood down. I long for the daylight shining off the stones of Asgard. After we pass several mountains, the dampened sound of clanging metal grows louder, accompanied by the bubbling of water.

Ahead, I spot a waterfall several feet tall, the freshness of the water a welcome scent after the rotting corpses of Niflheim. "That's not a bad sight. At least we have a waterfall to look at." As we approach, the muffled clanging of metal grows louder.

Elan huffs along our bond. *Except it's full of swords again. Can't you hear them banging against each other?*

Squinting in the darkness, I spot several flashes of silver, and my heart sinks. "I can. I just didn't realize it was coming from the waterfall. I thought only the other river was full of swords."

Thor clears his throat. "I have read there are a few different rivers in the under realms that are full of swords."

Britta groans. "Lovely! They really mustn't want people swimming in the under realms. They have several full of swords and one full of venomous snakes." Her body visibly shakes. "I wonder how they freshen up down here?"

"Excuse me." A lady's voice interrupts our

musing over the rivers. I glance up to see a middle-aged woman walking along the path toward us. Her face has a soft, round beauty, and her blond hair flows past her shoulders. She continues, not waiting for our answer. "Are you from the living?"

Thor twitches his hammer handle as if unsure how to respond. "Yes."

She clasps her hands, and her eyes widen. "Fantastic! I haven't seen anybody alive for such a long time." Hope washes over her face, and I'm not sure why until she asks, "Can you take a message up to my husband?"

At first, Thor splays his legs and crosses his arms, then he tries another approach and places a gentle hand on her shoulder. "I'm sorry. We are unable to carry any messages. But you know, you should be able to take that message to him yourself."

Her eyes shine. "Really?"

"Yes," Thor says. "All you need to do is let your spirit travel to the surface or use someone close to him who can hear you pass on the message."

"Have you seen people do it before?" she asks.

Thor spreads his arms. "Of course! I hear people talking about ghostly visits all the time. Some swear they know who is visiting, and sometimes the people just have a feeling. I don't know whether the strength of the message has to do with the ghost or the receiver." He rubs her on the back of the shoulders.

The woman's eyes shine brighter. "Thank you." She turns in the other direction as though ready to experiment.

Thor clasps his hands behind his back and grins. "Now she has something to achieve."

I shake my head. "I hope you don't tell that to all of the spirits who want to pass on messages to living loved ones. Then we'll have a major haunting on our hands."

Thor chuckles. "I guess you're right."

We pass through more gatherings of souls, searching every face for a sign of Balder. The search would be easier if we knew whether he still possessed his ability to shine even in the underworld. After searching several groups, we come up empty-handed.

Sick of wasting time, Hildr approaches a group of souls. "Excuse me. We are looking for someone."

A man with a lazy eye asks, "Who are you looking for? Maybe one of us knows them."

"It's worth a try." Thor shrugs and moves next to Hildr. "We're looking for Balder, the god of light."

A lady with long blond hair and a flawless complexion gasps. "Oh yes, that was such a shock.

He's the invincible god. Everything swore it wouldn't harm him. Yet he's down here in Helheim."

Thor's blue eyes light up. "So, you know where he is?"

The lady's blond hair swings as she nods. "I've heard that he remains within Hel's vicinity. It seems that because he is well-liked and he's a god, she has given him an important position. She determined to keep him close."

Thor fiddles with his hammer's handle, and he seems to be trying to contain his hope. "Can you point us in the right direction?"

"That's easy." She scans the horizon, her eyes focusing on an unusual dull beam of light cutting through the darkness. "Over there." She points. "That light in the distance is from Balder. Even in death, he shines."

Britta groans. "But that's so far."

The lady smiles as if she understands. "Helheim is a large realm. In reality, it's only a couple of mountains away. Just follow the light."

The anxiety in Thor's eyes softens. "At least that gives us a bearing. Thank you for your assistance."

"My pleasure." She grasps Thor's wrist. "Although, I would love for you to do something for me when you leave Helheim."

Thor freezes on the spot, his face awash with apprehension. "What would that be?"

"I would like you to pass on a message to my children."

Thor's shoulders visibly stiffen, and when his chuckle finally comes, it's nervous. "It's not usually something I would do. However, you did help us out." He glances in my direction, pleading for help.

I shake my head at his terror over a simple task. Here is a god who can bring down giants yet passing on a simple message from a deceased to a loved one has him shaking in his boots.

"Perhaps I'll be able to help you with this," I say.

The lady smiles. "A female touch may be better."

I didn't have the heart to tell the lady I don't have any motherly instincts, but I'm sure I can call on Eir if need be. I grab Eir's hand, and without a word, the peaceful Valkyrie seems to know what I need.

Chapter Seventeen

After bidding the lady farewell, we travel up the path, following it for quite some time before coming to a crossroad.

"Oh, Vanir! Now which way?" Hildr stands in the middle, her fists planted on her hips. "I'm so tired of walking that I don't want to take a wrong turn."

Drogon nudges her, careful not to stab her with one of his horns. *I vote we fly. It would be much quicker than trudging on foot.*

Yes, Elan agrees. *We should have left Sleipnir behind and carried Thor on our backs.*

Thor crosses his arms. "Sleipnir is swift and strong. That's why Odin lent him to me. He's much more robust than any other horse."

Then why didn't you tell us before? Tanda groans. *We could've saved a lot of time.*

Eir comes to Thor's defense. "We've only just come to a part where we could see far enough in front of us for Thor to ride the horse. After our ordeal in Niflheim, it's hard to think straight let alone ride for a while."

"You're right, Eir." Thor places a hand on the Valkyrie's shoulder. "But now we're ready. I'll ride the horse, and you lot fly. The dragons can direct me through mind speak."

Happy to get off our feet, the riders mount their dragons, and Zildryss hooks himself around Eir's shoulders.

Thor climbs onto Sleipnir's back. The eight-legged horse shuffles his feet on the spot, showing off the taut muscles under his cream coat. "There shouldn't be anything in this realm that will attack me. As far as I understand, no one here is a murderer. That's only on Niflheim."

Naga spreads his wings, exposing the little white stars on the membrane underneath. *Then let's get started. Naga's tired of walking on the ground, and Naga wants to get out of this dark realm. It's spooky.* His big blue eyes focus on a small group of souls behind us. *Even if these beings are happy, Naga doesn't want to come here.*

Eir slips a hand under one of Naga's blue scales in front of her saddle. "Then that would mean that you would have to die during a battle, Naga."

If Naga dies by Eir's side, then Naga is happy. Naga

wants to go where Eir goes. His body bends as he focuses large, passionate eyes on the rider sitting on his back.

"Oh, Naga!" Eir chimes. "That's so sweet! I want to spend my afterlife with you also."

The blue dragon's eyes light up with joy, and he smiles before pushing off. The air around us billows, and the other dragons push into the sky, following Naga's lead. It's almost comforting to feel the rise and fall of our flight in time with the beat of Elan's wings. The ground remains under the cover of darkness, barely visible at the lower height. I slip my hand underneath one of Elan's scales, touching her soft flesh and channeling into her dragon sight. There are still some pockets of mist on Helheim, yet they're nothing compared to the blinding fog on Niflheim. We fly through one of the pockets, and a layer of mist wets my face, chilling my cheeks in the cold air.

Balder's light shines dimly up ahead. Even though it is only a couple of mountain ranges away, it is still quite a distance. His dull glow provides an abnormal light for this realm, yet it's the kind of beacon we need to find him through the darkness.

After we've had a few minutes in the air, the chilly breeze has numbed my cheeks, and I slap each one lightly, trying to stimulate blood circulation in them. At least the air is fresh and not filled with the smell of rotting corpses like in Niflheim. It's hard to believe that Muspelheim and Niflheim are on the same level as Helheim. Muspelheim's heat is unbearable, as is the coldness and stench on Niflheim. Shaking my head, I pull my concentration back to Helheim and our task at hand. Thor remains at the crossroads, waiting for my instructions. Still using Elan's dragon sight, I follow the path as far as I can to assess which one is the fastest for Thor to travel.

I pass my findings on to Elan, sending a feeling along our bond.

I see the one, Elan says then repeats the directions to Thor. *The path on the left is much shorter than the path on the right. It passes along the river for quite some distance, and there is a valley we can't see into, but we won't let you out of our sight.*

Thor waves his acknowledgment up to Elan and guides Sleipnir along the river. Now that the horse is galloping at full speed, I can see why Odin thought it would be a good idea to send him with Thor. The horse's pale coat is easier to keep track of against the night sky of Helheim. His coat shimmers under occasional patches of lighter sky. The horse is fast, faster than any other horse that we have seen. The dragons need to circle back occasionally to keep up with the horse's progress. Still, the eight-legged horse is fast.

Drogon, Naga, and Tanda hover above Elan as I

watch over Thor, making sure nothing in Helheim attacks him. All is going well until Thor reaches the valley and doesn't come up the other side. Elan circles back to find him on the ground and standing next to Sleipnir, who dances nervously between two mountain ranges.

The god of thunder's knees are bent as though bracing himself on the ground, and his arms shield his head as rocks topple off the mountain ranges.

The ground is shaking again, Elan sighs. *Nidhogg must be chewing on Yggdrasil again. I had hoped he would stop that bad habit after meeting us.*

The ground shakes another time. After meeting the wyvern, I understand how his simple mind can't deal with the insults other than by destroying the world tree, another threat to the worlds and one that we will have to work on.

"Elan, can you please lower so we can check to see if Thor is okay?"

The majestic golden dragon drops close to the ground and circles my leader.

Is all okay, Thor? Elan asks.

Thor follows Elan's progress as he responds, "Sleipnir's legs seem to be shaking, and I didn't realize why until I climbed off him."

A loud crack captures my attention, and I search unsuccessfully for the source. "What was that?"

Elan studies the surrounding area, her wings freezing for a split second. *Dragon scales!*

I focus on her vision through our bond and spot an enormous boulder on top of the mountain range, balancing precariously over Thor's path.

Look out! Elan calls.

Thor grabs Sleipnir's reins and drags the horse backward. Both god and horse run so fast that their feet skid on the dirt when they stop. A loud *thud* captures Thor's attention, and he faces forward to find the boulder completely blocking their path between the two mountain ranges.

He wipes his brow with his sleeve. "That was close." He huffs as though at a private joke. "That would have been ironic, dying in Helheim." His body rocks with a shiver. "That would mean I would've had to stay here permanently."

Elan circles above. *It's good that it missed you,* she huffs. *However, we have another problem.*

Thor cranes his neck and looks at her. "What's that?"

"The only way around it is to go back to the cross-roads before you turned left."

Thor's shoulders sag. "Oh Vanir! That's not good."

Chapter Eighteen

Spinning once, twice, three times, Thor grunts and swings his hammer, letting it fly straight at the boulder. Shards of rock shatter around the point of impact, and the hammer returns into the god of thunder's hand. Each time with a mighty grunt, Thor repeats this, his result a shower of rock.

Elan circles a final time and lands on the other side of Sleipnir, the horse showing more intelligence than the god by remaining away from the impact of the shattering rocks.

From Elan's back, I call to my leader. "Ah, Thor. What are you doing?"

Thor tosses his hand in the direction of the boulder. "I'm chipping my way through the rock. Can't you see that?"

With another spin and an ample grunt, he releases Mjolnir directly at the boulder again. The large rock releases a few more shards, the impact chipping a minuscule amount off the top and the results repeating with each attempt. To get past this boulder, he has a long way to go.

I push my lips to one side. "Yes, I can see that. And you're doing a good job," I say hesitantly. "But this is going to take forever."

Thor catches Mjolnir another time and pauses briefly, his chest heaving and irritation oozing from every pore. "And so is turning around and going back where we came."

I observe the large boulder and the tiny pile of shattered rocks at its base. "I understand your frustration. But think on this for a moment instead of just using your aggression. Maybe we can work something out."

Thor spins, rereleasing his hammer and breaking off another small amount of rock. "Or maybe I can just keep chipping away while you're doing the thinking."

Cringing, I block my head with my arms as a cascade of stones topples over us. "The dragons can take you over."

Thor catches his hammer again and throws it. "Yes, but they can't take the horse over too. I must return with Sleipnir, or my father will be upset."

Elan flinches as another shower of rocks topples over us. *He's got a point.* She squints as a large *crack* comes again a few seconds later. *But if we had something strong enough to hook under the horse, perhaps we could carry Sleipnir over with two dragons.*

"Call the others down, Elan, and let's put our heads together to see what we can use or if they have a better idea."

I climb off Elan, my mind lost in thought, trying to think of something that would be strong enough to hold the horse between two dragons. It isn't very far to the other side of the boulder. Still, carrying something the size of a horse is going to require strength. If we don't get Sleipnir over the boulder, it could add another half day's travel to our trip.

The breeze brushes up my back, and my hands automatically grasp for my coat, but I'm not wearing it. It's still in my saddlebag. After stepping up on the stirrup, I yank it out of the pack and pull it on, wrapping the dragon-scale-covered leather around me. My hand catches on one of the dragon scales sewn on the outside, and a thought occurs to me.

The strong leather has never let me down. It has always protected me—like Elan and her family. This coat is made from their scales and a tough animal hide from the dragon wastelands.

The thumping of the dragons landing near Elan pulls me back to my surroundings.

"What's up?" Hildr climbs off Drogon, and the other Valkyries follow suit.

Still fiddling with the edges of my coat, I say, "I need your help to think of something strong enough to carry Sleipnir between two dragons and over that boulder."

Britta flinches as more shards of rocks shower over us. "Over that big boulder."

My mouth forms a thin line. "Yes. It is slowly getting smaller thanks to Thor, but it has a long way to go."

Elan blows steam over Thor, expressing her annoyance at his persistence in shattering the rock and the mess he is making. *We need to carry the horse across the boulder. I can take Thor, but the only way I can carry a horse without hurting it by myself is if it is upside down. He's not going to like that. My talons will hurt him, trying to carry him any other way.*

A frown creases Eir's forehead. "How do you suggest we do it, then?"

"How about this?" Hildr shoots several magic bolts at it, smashing off about the same amount of rock as a blow from Mjolnir. Britta and Eir join her, and I also have a few attempts, but my energy hasn't recovered from the loss of part of my soul to Modgud. Even the other Valkyries' energy depletes quickly.

As the four Valkyries puff, attempting to get their energy back, Thor throws his hammer again, and a shard of stone hits my cheek. When I pull my fingers away, blood covers them.

Thor looks guilty. "Sorry."

I shrug. "It's okay, I guess."

Britta dusts off a few stones that got caught on her sleeve. "We should have put up our protective barrier by now."

I pull off my coat. "We should have, but I'm exhausted." Even pulling my jacket off takes too much energy. "I think we should try my other idea."

"What's that?" Britta asks.

"We hook my coat under Sleipnir's belly and have a dragon on each side clasping the coat."

Thor pauses his throwing. "We do what?"

I spin the coat so the inside is exposed to them. "As you can see, the inside of my coat is made of leather. It's strong and sturdy." I pull at it, emphasizing the point. "Although it's not big, we can stretch it under the horse's stomach, and the dragons can grab the edges. Hopefully, it's as tough as the saddles, only more flexible."

Tanda sniffs the cloak. *It's worth a try. Perhaps all four of us can do it.*

Elan shakes her head. *No. Forget that. It would be*

too small with the four of us that close to each other. We wouldn't be able to fly.

Drogon sticks his head into the center, his horns on his forehead bunched together. He snorts. *It'll have to be Elan and myself.*

Elan tilts her head to one side. *Hmm. We'll have to keep low, though. The leather is strong, but the horse is heavy. I would hate for the leather to snap and Sleipnir to break some legs.*

Another smashing sound pulls our attention to the boulder. Tanda scowls at the rocks that rain down on her. *Well, at least with Thor's and the Valkyries' effort, the boulder is flattened slightly.* She towers over Thor, giving him an intimidating glare and sizing him up when he catches the hammer again. *I could carry you over while Drogon and Elan attempt to take Sleipnir over.*

Without waiting for Thor's response, Tanda lowers for Britta to climb on, and she flies her over to the other side of the boulder. Naga and Eir follow with Zildryss wrapped around Eir's shoulder, remaining by Britta's side as Tanda returns for Thor.

The red dragon huffs steam over Thor. *I should really shake you up a little for all the showers of stones I've received because of you. But I won't. I'm too nice.*

When she steams him again, he smirks at her. "I know you like it."

Tanda grabs Thor's jerkin in her teeth, throws the

god on her back, and laughs at Thor's pale face. *Just like I know you liked that*. She whips her tail, which ends in a white ball of fluff, and projects into the air, carrying Thor out of our sight.

Chuckling at the dragon's win over the god, I lay my cloak on the ground with the scales facing down so they won't dig into the horse's hide. Hildr leads Sleipnir, poises him over the cloak, and places a comforting hand on his nose as the dragons move to either side and grab hold of the cloak. With a united push of their wings, the dragons lift, hooking the horse underneath and lifting it off the ground.

Hildr releases Sleipnir's reins and stands by me. As the dragons rise, I cross my fingers, hoping all will go as planned. The dragons lift Sleipnir higher, their wings pumping strenuously in an attempt to hold the package steady until they are only a few feet away from the top of the boulder. Sleipnir glances down, his eyes wide with panic, then he kicks. Elan and Drogon fight to keep him steady and almost reach the top. Then the sound that we all dread reaches our ears. *Rip*.

Chapter Nineteen

The horse whinnies, and the dragons struggle to lower him to the ground before the cloak rips further. Yet they're too late. When the leather tears again, the dragons drop quickly, and a *snap* follows their land. Sleipnir's eyes widen, and he tumbles to the ground, his struggles to stand unfruitful.

Hildr runs to the horse's side, her hands running nimbly over the Sleipnir's leg, stopping when she spots the lower leg lying at an odd angle.

She wipes her forehead on the sleeve of her black uniform. "It's broken." She brushes the horse's snout and rubs it gently between its wide eyes.

After moving in front of Sleipnir, I gently run my fingers over the broken limb, feeling for the exact point of the break. The horse stiffens as I near the painful spot, and he tosses his head in my direction, watching my every move. Hildr scratches him around the ears, running her hand gently along his neck, eventually calming the horse enough for it to lower its head to the ground. When I touch the sore again, his head flings up, his eyes wide.

Even though I understand the horse's distress, it's making it impossible for him to heal. I need backup. "Elan and Drogon, can you two please hold the horse still? Straightening the bones will probably hurt him and feel odd as the bones return to their positions. I also need him to remain still so I can heal him. The last thing I need is for him to take off halfway through the mending."

Without responding, Elan and Drogon lie next to Sleipnir and slowly lay their heads across the horse's body as though using him as a pillow. Elan lies over the neck, and Drogon carefully directs his numerous horns away from the horse as he lays a third of his body over the horse's flank.

"Clever dragons," I say, realizing what they're doing. The horse would have a tough time lifting the weight off so he can get up. "That's one way of pinning him down without hurting him."

Sleipnir attempts to move, his eyes wide when he can't get up. He thrashes his legs. Hildr sits opposite me and grasps his injured leg, holding it still. "It's okay, Sleipnir," she croons. "We're only here to help."

She talks as though the horse can understand her and strokes his snout.

The horse snickers, and in that moment of distraction, I quickly yank the bone into the correct position. Sleipnir panics and struggles, but the only movement he can make doesn't affect the leg. Several times, he attempts to stand, but the dragons' weight pins him to the ground. After two attempts, he mellows as the shock wears off, eventually lying still.

Smoothly, I run a hand up the side of his snout, calming magic humming through my palm and entering the horse's body. "I'm sorry, big guy. I had to do that. It has to be straight before I mend it. Trust me. I feel your pain. It has happened to me as well." Gradually, I work my way closer to the wound, watching as the skin grows over the hole created by the protruding bone, and the fractured bone solidifies under my touch. I stop only when I'm sure it is healed. Even then, I give it some more healing magic.

I gaze at Drogon, still lying across the horse's rear, then at Elan, her head resting on the horse's neck. "Okay, I think I'm done. The leg should be healed."

Elan groans, slowly rising off Sleipnir. *That's a pity. It was quite comfortable resting my head on the horse. He's like a nice little cushion.* She smiles, looking more ferocious than friendly, and Drogon rises with her.

They tower over the horse on each side as he springs to his feet and trots in a circle, tossing his head. The eight-legged horse moves with grace as he prances, testing the strength of his leg.

The warmth of satisfaction floods over me. "He seems healed."

Hildr pushes her mouth to one side. "Yes, but the next step is trying to get him over that boulder."

Drogon throws something at me, and it lands at my feet. *Sorry about your coat. It looks like it's seen better days.*

Sadness fills me. I loved that dragon-scale coat. Tamping down the deep hope rising inside of me that the damage isn't bad, I stoop down to grab it. The hard scales press into my palm as I stretch it out and spot the massive rip up the center of the back.

My heart beats with the rhythm of excitement. "It looks like it can be fixed." I run my fingers along the torn edge. "This should be enough leather for me to be able to sew it back together." When I raise my eyes to look at my friends, I catch sight of the boulder again, and my shoulders slump. "But it's not going to help get Sleipnir over the boulder. It won't be strong enough."

We turn our attention to the boulder. Sleipnir's excited trots drown out my thoughts as he prances and kicks past us, showing off his eight working legs.

The stirrups swing from his saddle, still strapped around his torso, the robust straps hooking under the horse's belly.

I rub my chin. "The other way you could carry him over is by his saddle."

Hildr shakes her head. "I don't think that will work, Kara. Although the leather straps are thick, I don't think they'll be strong enough. They are designed to strap the saddle to the horse, not pick up a whole horse."

Elan slumps to her backside and groans. *What are we going to do? There is no other way to carry the horse over. Our talons would hurt Sleipnir, and I'm sure he won't put up with being hung upside down between us.*

I certainly wouldn't. Drogon snorts out steam. *That would require a lot of trust. Even though I have faith with all of the dragons here, I would have to be almost dead to allow them to do it.* He watches the horse prance around some more. *And this horse is definitely not almost dead. He's going to struggle the whole way.*

The clip-clopping of the horse's hooves continues, occasionally giving off a higher pitch when the hooves hit stones. A soft breeze brushes my hair across my face, and I tie it into a ponytail. The chilly breeze continues against my face and down my neck, and despite it being torn, I slide on my jacket and welcome its warmth.

Hildr rubs her upper arms. "I'm not sure this is possible, but do you think we can carry the horse over with our combined magic?"

I frown. "I don't know. If we can lift it, I'd be concerned that we'll run out of energy when the horse is stuck in the air. If Sleipnir falls again, we won't have enough energy to heal him."

Hildr scratches her temple. "Maybe the dragons can fly near him and catch his saddle if we run out of energy. Surely it will hold long enough for them to place him gently on the other side."

I worry my lip. "Let's see how we feel lifting him a little way. If we feel okay after lifting him a few feet, we'll continue." I turn to Elan and Drogon. "Can you two please remain by his side, just in case?"

Elan stretches her wings. *Ready when you are.*

Reaching out with our palms facing the horse, Hildr and I coax Sleipnir gently with our magic. We lift the horse a couple of feet, and instantly, the magic seeps from my body. Wondering whether it's just me because of the weakness still throbbing in me from the partial soul removal, I connect eyes with Hildr. She shakes her head. Disappointment rises in me as we carefully return the horse to the ground. Lifting a large animal is more difficult than I'd thought.

Hildr's chest heaves. "We can't do it. It's too hard."

Resting, I keel over with my palms planted on my knees. "There is only one way left, and I don't like the chances of the horse staying still."

Standing straight and stretching her hips forward, Hildr asks, "Can we knock it out with magic?"

Dumbfounded, I blink at her. "It's not a stupid idea, but it sounds barbaric." I massage my temples. "Although I'm worried that it will hurt the horse."

Hildr shrugs. "Then you can heal him again. As you said, we've run out of options." She paces around the front of Sleipnir. "If you can't heal him afterward, then Eir should be able to. After all, peaceful magic is her thing."

Clenching my teeth, I grind them together. "I should be able to heal him, but I don't like the sound of this." The permanent frown is giving me a headache. "I'm not used to playing with minds. I might kill Sleipnir by mistake."

Hildr tsks. "Then I'll do it. I don't want to hurt him either. Unless you have a different plan."

A few moments pass as I attempt to think of a better way to get Sleipnir over the boulder, and dejection washes over me. I shake my head. "I don't. Although I'm still not keen on doing it."

Hildr leans to one hip. "Then that settles it. I'll be the bad one. You can be the good one who heals him later."

Her footsteps crunch on the loose stones as she approaches the horse, and I pull at the edge of my uniform, ringing it in my hands in an attempt to rid myself of stress and worry. Not only do I not like hurting animals, but this is also Odin's horse, and if something happens to him, we will never hear the end of this, if not be exiled.

Hildr approaches the horse slowly as though he's a friend, her demeanor calm, and she hushes him with soothing tones. It feels like a betrayal. Sleipnir has faith in us. We healed him earlier, yet now we're about to harm him. The fact that we are in Helheim makes it worse, as though we brought him here and he will never leave.

Just as Hildr's palms reach Sleipnir's temples, the ground shakes violently, and I wonder whether it's Nidhogg gnawing at the roots of Yggdrasil again. Hildr's eyes are as wide as mine as we search for something untoward, but we come up empty. Except the boulder is shrinking, slowly sinking into the ground until it disappears completely, and the path resurfaces. I gape through the passage, and my jaw drops.

Chapter Twenty

Disbelief washes over me. Without any warning and after we've had so much heartache, the entrance is open.

"What just happened?" Hildr turns her back on Sleipnir and gazes through the opening.

With smiles on their faces, Thor, Eir, Britta, Tanda, and Naga block the path on the other side of the gap. My sight travels to the ground. In front, the tiny form of Zildryss sits in the middle of the path. His tail arches over his head, a position he holds after he has struck the ground with it like a scorpion.

Elan's shoulders slump. *You've got to be kidding me!*

Drogon clears his throat. *I think it's more like we're the clowns who were doing the kidding. None of us thought about the little dragon being able to bury things in the ground.* He grumbles. *I mean, how stupid! If he can bury giant trolls in the earth, surely he can sink a big rock.*

"It would've saved a lot of hassle," Hildr says. "I feel so stupid."

Eir chuckles, scooping up the little dragon then snuggling him within her palms. "That makes all of us. We keep forgetting about how special this little guy is."

Unfazed, Zildryss peeks out through Eir's fingers, his tongue lashing from one eye to the other.

Thor marches to Sleipnir and grabs the horse's reins. "At least we can go now. Did everything go okay on this side?" He strokes the horse's face. "We thought you lot would have been over by now."

"No, it didn't go okay." I hold up my torn coat. "We had a bit of a mishap. The dragons tried to lower Sleipnir gently, but the tear grew too fast, and he broke his leg."

Thor stops pulling Sleipnir and assesses his eight legs.

"But don't worry." I hold out a hand. "All his legs are fine. The injury has been healed. Your father isn't going to be upset. That is, if he doesn't find out."

Thor grins sheepishly. "Hey, if it's not broken, we don't need to tell him." He grabs the reins again and pulls Sleipnir through the opening then climbs onto the horse's back. "Let's get the show moving, shall we?" Without waiting for our response, he taps his heels lightly on the horse's ribs and continues down the path.

We climb onto our dragons and take to the sky, with Zildryss tucked around Eir's neck, and head toward Balder's dull light in the distance. Thankfully, the rest of the journey is unobstructed, and Sleipnir moves quickly along the path without the need for guidance. The trip to the light takes longer than I expected, and I'm surprised by Helheim's size.

Elan circles back a couple of times and checks on Thor's progress and safety. I slide my hand under Elan's scale and connect with her dragon sight. The darkness of Helheim creeps under my skin yet fails to bring the ominous threat of the thick fog of Niflheim. Sunshine will be a welcome relief when we leave this realm. Even though the dead don't seem upset, I think the darkness would lodge in my soul and cast me into a deep depression. It's exceptionally gloomy.

When we near the end of the path, the dragons land and wait for Sleipnir to arrive. A wide river creates an island, and in the middle, Balder's light continues to shine dimly. A bridge reaches across the water, but I'm relieved to find that this bridge isn't a floating golden bridge operated by Modgud. Even so, as we cross over, my nerves fire on all ends, waiting to be ambushed by an almost skeletal giant. Instead, several souls hold gifts as they cross the bridge toward the light. Their demeanor is more one of worship than of terror.

A woman carrying a large gift captures my attention. The moment her feet touch the ground at the end of the bridge, she treads up a hill lined with stairs. I hasten to watch her progress, observing her as she climbs what appears to be an unending tower of stairs. Craning my neck, I catch sight of a figure at the top who seems to be a woman yet unlike any other woman that I have seen before. Although stories have spread throughout Asgard, I am still not prepared for what I see. The woman at the top looks as though she is two different people cut in half lengthwise. One side of the person is beautiful, with perfect skin, full lips, and long, luscious hair. On the other, the skin is dry and shriveled, sucking against the woman's bones as though it is nonexistent, making her look like a skeleton. I squint, attempting to get a better look. Or maybe it is a skeleton. A long black gown falls to the woman's feet as she sits on a throne made from bones.

"All hail, great goddess, Hel." A man behind us falls to his knees and bows, his forehead striking the ground and arms extended in front of him.

Shocked by what I see, I sidestep away from the

man and hurry after the woman bearing the gift before halting at the bottom of the stairs. Her long blond hair falls down her back, and her thin garment swooshes around her ankles as she holds her gift high, making sure the woman at the top can see it.

She pauses several steps below, holding the gift higher. "A gift for my appreciation, high goddess." The lady topples to her knees and bows, her posture an imitation of the man's. While she places the package among the abundant offerings, some topple over.

It looks like she doesn't even want the gifts. Elan's voice is a welcome distraction, and I nod.

A mixture of red sky shining from Muspelheim and the dull gleam of Balder's light illuminates Hel, outlining her thin silhouette.

Eir whispers in my ear, "That's a bit creepy."

I squint to study Hel further. There are almost too many gifts on the stairs, prohibiting anyone from reaching the top. Then I confirm that the skin on her skeleton is nonexistent, and the eye on that side is missing. The skeletal side lacks the luscious hair that flows down to the shoulder on the living side. I had heard that Hel wanted to move to Helheim because she is more comfortable being around the dead. As I behold her, this makes sense.

My eyes fall to her feet and see the same two-sided appearance. Healthy skin covers one foot while the other is bone.

Britta shifts closer. "This isn't what I was expecting."

"Me neither," I agree. "I was expecting more terror among the souls." I glance around at the souls nearby. They seem to lack worry and distress. Strangely, they seem content.

The woman remains in the prone position, and we ascend the stairs, carefully pushing aside some gifts to give us a path to walk through.

We'll wait here, Elan says. *If you need us, we'll be there in a couple of flaps.*

Thanks, Elan, I respond through our bond.

The clack of the dragons' talons and Sleipnir's hooves on the stones at the base follows us on our ascension. It is a long way to the top, and even my Valkyrie-trained legs burn from the exertion.

When we reach the final ten steps, we pause. Something lands on my shoulders, and I jump, letting go of my breath only when I spot the lilac scales of Zildryss.

Thor bows his head as if in respect. "It's lovely to see you again, Hel. I see this realm is treating you well, and you are ruling it wisely."

Hel taps the long black claws protruding from her skeletal fingers, and the empty eye socket seems to stare at us more intently than her fleshy eye. "What would you know of how I rule this realm, god of thunder?" Her tone is neutral, showing no signs of emotion.

Thor indicates the realm behind him and all the gifts littering the stairs. "I can tell by the way your subjects treat you."

Hel raises her chin. "And I suppose you think that I have you to thank for that."

The god holds out his hand. "No, that isn't what I was implying. I hoped that your life here is better than the one you had while trapped in a cave. My father is the one who sent you here."

"Yes. It is better." She stares down her nose at him. "And why are you here? You're not dead." She observes each of us, and the fleshy side of her face turns stony. "None of you are dead. You shouldn't be here."

Thor presses his palms together. "We have come to ask for you to release Balder. Although I have not seen him yet, I believe he is here. He didn't die in an honorable way."

"Ha. Typical," Hel scoffs. "You only pay me heed when you want something."

"No, that isn't true. We figured that you wanted to be left alone to rule your realm the way you wished. Please, if you have met Balder, you will know that he deserves an honorable afterlife in Valhalla. Or return him to the land of the living so that he has another chance."

I squirm under Hel's gaze. The uneasy feeling makes the silence extend into a long, drawn-out pause.

"No." Hel's face sets in determination.

Chapter Twenty-One

All thoughts vanish from my mind as the shock sets in. All that we went through to get here was for nothing. Hel isn't going to release Balder so that he may live in the honorable afterlife. The goddess didn't even give us a chance to explain anything. By the looks on my friends' faces, I can tell each of the Valkyries want to say something to change her mind, but they know that it's best to leave the diplomacy to Thor.

The god of thunder opens his mouth a couple of times only to close it again when words fail to come. Eventually, he manages to get past his apparent shock. Spreading his arms wide with his palms facing the goddess, he sighs and neutralizes his expression. "I understand, and I respect your decision. But we beg of you to please reconsider. Perhaps there is something that we can trade for Balder. Something that you may want in order to release him. You are the only one with the power to release him." Thor rubs his palms on the sides of his pants. "As you may know, Balder is a kind, giving god. Everyone on Asgard is mourning his death. It has been such a shock. After everything promising not to harm him, the jokes and the gods' playful attempts to injure him have gone on for too long. We believed we could do anything to him, and he wouldn't be harmed. We were wrong. The crack in Frigg's plan was penetrated, and now Balder pays the price."

When Hel only stares at Thor, her face unmoving, the god persists, trying another tactic.

"Please don't punish Balder for Asgard's capture of your father. I know this has brought spite and anger from Fenrir and Jormungandr and has angered you in the past. I understand you may still be upset because we have entrapped your father again and that this may affect your decision on this matter."

A strange expression passes over Hel's face, and the fleshy side of her mouth raises in what seems like a smile. "Is that what you think?" A hint of laughter shakes her words.

Thor looks dumbfounded. "Well, we have considered it. As I said, we know that your siblings are upset because of his capture." He stammers, seeming baffled by her humor.

"And when was the last time you saw my

siblings?" She glances at Sleipnir. "My monster siblings. The ones from Angrboda."

"We saw Fenrir not long before Balder died. He was so upset over your father's capture that we entrapped him the day of Balder's death. He left us no choice. He had become too violent because of Loki's capture."

Hel chuckles a strange sound, crisp and husky at the same time. "That might have been the case at that time, but since then, my father has escaped again."

Thor's face turns blank before his brow furrows. "What do you mean?"

Hel sits back on her throne of bones, crosses her skeletal leg over the fleshy one, and rests her hands on her lap. "Who do you think the old woman was who guided the mistletoe into Balder's heart?"

The color drains from Thor's face. "Was it Loki?" His voice is barely louder than a whisper.

She laughs. "Who else in Asgard do you think is conniving enough to extract the information out of Frigg, Balder's mother, on what could harm him, then also manage to guide the dejected blind brother to throw the spear made of mistletoe, the only potent item, straight into Balder's heart?"

"But there haven't been reports of him escaping." Thor runs a hand through his thick auburn hair. "There would have been reports by now. Someone would've seen him missing." A deep frown creases his forehead as he continues with his questions. "And how could he escape? Did someone help him?"

Hel pushes up and stands, her skeletal side working as though laced with muscles.

She paces, her long black dress flowing smoothly around her flesh and looking more rugged around the harsh contours of her bony side. After a few steps, she pauses and gazes at my leader with her fleshy side more prominent. Her eye is curious yet also demeaning. "Think about it, god. Think about what Loki is." Her tone is harsher than it was previously.

I suck in a breath, expelling the words in a whisper loud enough for Thor to hear before I can stop myself. "A shape-shifter." The words are dragged out and slow. "He's a shape-shifter." I work my palm against my forehead. "How did we miss that?"

Disbelief and confusion fill Thor's eyes, then they land on me. "We didn't miss it." He shakes his head. "We know he's a shape-shifter. But how was he the old woman?"

"He can change into any shape, and because of this, he can escape any location as long as it isn't magically bound." I rub my aching temples. "Did the gods magically bind him the last time they secured him?"

Thor's face pales, brightening his freckles. "I don't believe they did." His pained expression passes from Hel to me. "So, what Ratatoskr said was true. Loki was the woman."

Slow, tedious clapping echoes down from above. It's not the usual slap of flesh on flesh but rather the hollow sound of a fleshy palm slapping against a fleshy leg buffed by fabric. "He finally worked it out. In your defense, though, I guess they didn't call you the god of brains, did they? Thunder and temper are more like it." She sits on her throne and crosses her fleshy leg over her skeletal one. "Let me explain it to you. Because I have known that my father can escape quite readily this time, I haven't come to punish you or Asgard. I haven't even sent any minions from any realm to go against Asgard and attack you." She sits back on her chair and kicks the crossed leg. "Despite what you think, I have been sitting here peacefully."

Thor rubs the back of his neck and looks at her sheepishly. "Oh. We appreciate it."

Hel's mouth forms a straight line. "Of course you do. It's not like last time you captured my father and I convinced Surt to send the lava monster. Although he didn't need much convincing, because he wanted access to Freya. I just helped him with an idea."

Thor hitches up his pants at the waist. "So, since you aren't angry with us, why are you holding Balder, even though you can release him?"

She shrugs her bony shoulder nonchalantly. "He is dead. Plain and simple. He died a dishonorable death, according to Asgard. He belongs in this realm." She lifts the skirt of her dress slightly, read-justing it over her legs.

We rise a couple of steps, and the beauty of Hel's fleshy side shocks me. Her eyelashes are long and dark, framing a deep-chocolate eye. Her slim figure is accentuated by the dull light shining behind her, the one we were led to believe was Balder, yet we still haven't laid eyes on him.

Thor's eyes fix on the light accentuating Hel's form. "Where is Balder?"

Hel flips her hand over her shoulder at the dull glow behind her, nonchalantly. "Why? He is right behind me. Can't you see the light?"

Thor's bushy red eyebrows push together, crowding over his eyes. "But where behind you? We cannot see him."

Hel lifts the skirt of her black dress again and recrosses her legs in the opposite direction, the skeletal one over the normal and healthy one. "You can come and have a look if you like. He's in the little hollow in the ground behind me. I have given him this as a sanctuary so that he can settle in my world. There are too many souls wanting to be with him. Would you like to come and have a look?"

Slowly, Thor walks up the final steps, and the Valkyries follow close behind him. We move around Hel's eerie throne of bones and peer into the deep hole carved into the earth of Helheim. At the bottom, well below the height of his head, Balder is curled into the fetal position, sleeping soundly on a bed and snuggled under many blankets.

Chapter Twenty-Two

For the first time on Helheim, I can see all of my companions' faces clearly thanks to Balder's glowing skin. Britta sighs. "Isn't he beautiful?" She clutches her hands in front of her before her brow furrows slightly. "I don't remember his face glowing so spectacularly on Asgard."

Hel twists on her throne and gazes at us over the backrest. Her demeanor seems younger than her age in years, not much older than the Valkyries. "His light has always glowed brightly, dimmed only by Asgard's natural light." She indicates Helheim with her hand. "Here, his light will shine like a beacon, lighting the way through the dark."

Hildr taps a foot, her eyes distant. "That makes sense, but why is he down a hole?"

Hel lets out an exaggerated sigh. "Many of the dead here were doting over him. At one stage, they were smothering him. I created this space, tucked behind my throne, for protection to give him peace." Her eyes land on Thor. "As you mentioned, he was well-liked in Asgard, and I have heard of him. He deserves a good afterlife."

"Then when will you release him?" Thor asks, his pleading tone returning. "He was taken way too young. He needs a longer life."

Hel shifts uncomfortably on her throne. "As I said, he has died a death outside of battle. In your eyes, a dishonorable death. Because of that, this is where his home is."

Thor clenches his fists by his side. "Is there anything we can offer in return? I beg of you. His mother is beside herself weeping with grief, and all of Asgard mourns his passing."

A flash of lilac catches my eye, and Zildryss leaps off Eir's shoulder and glides into the hole before landing on Balder. He pitter-patters around the sleeping god's head, brushing his wing against his skin before resting against his neck. The tiny dragon presses his cheek against Balder's jaw, his eyes flying open a few moments later, and Zildryss's tongue lashes alternating eyes.

Curious, Hel pushes off her throne and saunters to our side. "What's going on down there?"

"I imagine that Zildryss is making sure Balder is okay," Eir says. "He's good like that."

"But he just looks like he's snuggling into the god," Hel argues.

"That's what he does. It's the way he communicates and assesses things. He always touches his scales directly to our skin." Eir's eyes are kind as she watches the little dragon. "I think it's adorable."

Hel huffs. "I knew the little dragon was special and made wise decisions, but I didn't know they could do that."

After a few moments, Zildryss climbs off Balder and onto his mattress, shakes himself off, then flies around the edges of the hole before rising slowly in a circular motion. His little chest heaves when he lands on Thor's shoulder and presses against his neck.

Thor expels a loud sigh. "Balder is fine. Hel has been taking good care of him, and he's in good health for a soul."

Hel crosses her arms, bony one over the fleshy one. "Of course he is."

Seeing the anger in her eyes, Thor says, "We didn't doubt it. But I'm sure you would understand that we needed to see if he is okay. After all, he did die."

When Hel's expression softens, Thor continues, "Please let him come back with us and give him a second chance to die an honorable death. You know he deserves it."

Hel moves farther away from the edge of the hole. "You act as though I should release people all the time."

"It's your realm, and you have the power to say who comes and who goes." Thor struggles to hide his frustration.

Hel nods, her long brunette hair falling over her fleshy face and hiding her eye from us momentarily. "That is true. But I'm not in the practice of sending back the dead."

Thor clasps his hands in front of him, imploring. "Please, I beg of you. Please consider releasing him back to Asgard, the land of the living."

The goddess's face remains unmoving, and he continues, "Name your price, and I'll do my best to pay it."

Hel strides back to her throne and sits before crossing her legs slowly, then she leans against the armrest and places her chin in the curve between her thumb and forefinger. She gazes down at the pile of discarded gifts, her eyes traveling to the dragons and horse. "That is quite an impressive entourage." Her eyes land on me. "It's an exceptional gift to be around a dragon."

I nod. "Yes, it is. I'm humbled that they chose us."

Her one fleshy eyebrow rises, and her eye lands

on Elan. "You even have an emperor dragon. Impressive. She must have seen something in you."

"She isn't mine. She is her own dragon. I have been honored that she has been my best friend for a few years now."

"They look quite vicious," Hel says.

We leave the side of the hole and move closer to the throne, and Eir stands next to me, staring at our dragon friends. "Despite their largeness, they are quite peaceful animals, even the one covered in horns."

"He does look rather aggressive. Are you trying to tell me he's a pussycat?" Hel purrs.

Eir shakes her head. "Oh no! He is far from it and will use his strength, horns, and other weapons when needed, just like the rest of them. But if you treat them with kindness, they are creatures of peace."

"As am I." With a sweeping hand, Hel indicates her realm. "Within this land, peace must be restored. Therefore, all the evildoers are sent to another part." She stands and circles her throne, gazing at the sleeping Balder with a blank face. Remaining without expression, she clasps her hands behind her back and moves to her throne then leans against the backrest from the side. Her eye travel over Eir and me then Britta, Hildr, and Thor. Her face softens when it lands on Zildryss, still on the god of thunder's shoulder.

"In order for me to release Balder, I have one request."

"Anything!" Thor says.

She casts him a discerning glance. "You should wait to hear the request before you agree to the conclusion. If one says it is only one task, it must not be assumed that it will be easy. The task could be a great mission or something that goes against your beliefs."

A mixture of agitation and desperation distorts Thor's face. Still, he holds his tongue and inclines his head. "You are most wise, Hel."

Speechless, Hel stares at Thor before bursting with laughter, a rough, coarse sound. "Being humble does not suit you, god of thunder. The pleading in your voice, it sounds so foreign, strange."

Thor blinks as if dumbfounded, looking torn over either yelling at Hel for being demeaning or swallowing his pride for his brother's sake. His Adam's apple bobs, then he washes all confliction away with a blank face. "Forgive me. It is not often that I need to be like this. I am a man of action. Being a diplomat isn't something I want to do."

She waves her skeletal arm at him dismissively. "The one task I wish to ask of you, and the only way I'm going to consider allowing Balder to return to Asgard, is this..." She paces slowly in front of her throne. "You need to get all beings of Yggdrasil realms to weep a tear for the death of Balder." She pauses in front of her throne and holds up a finger. "Then and only then will I return him to Asgard."

Hildr sneers. "Impossible!"

The goddess plants Hildr with a challenging glare and opens her mouth as if to speak.

"Done!" Thor interrupts whatever she was going to say.

A dimple grows on Hel's fleshy cheek. Her smile is puzzling. "Just as I expected. The predictable over-confident god of thunder. This is your true side." She sits and wriggles in her throne. "I don't think you realize just how difficult this mission will be. I need a tear from *everybody*, even the ones who haven't shed a tear since they were small children."

Thor scoffs. "It will be easy. Everybody loved Balder."

Hel pulls at her skirt, dropping it lower over her legs. The movement is strangely dainty yet also weird. "Then only time will tell."

Chapter Twenty-Three

Britta pulls her attention away from the sleeping god and pulls at the hem of her black leather top. "What happens to Balder if we don't succeed?"

A sly grin crosses Hel's face, accentuating the dimple on her fleshy side again. "Don't worry. I will take special care of him." She moves beside Britta, twirling her long dark strands of hair as she gazes at Balder's shining face. "I'll keep him company. I'm rather fond of him."

An unmistakable shiver runs down Thor's spine despite his clear attempt to hide it. I shift to stand next to him, and he mutters softly to me. "That's all kinds of disturbing."

Eir moves back to the rim of the hole, standing not far from the goddess. Her eyes are soft as she stares at the sleeping god and strokes Zildryss's back. "You've given us a huge task. We shall do our best to complete it. First, though, could you be kind enough to show us the way out of here?"

Hel moves past her throne, then her bony hand points in the direction opposite the one in which we came. "The Yggdrasil entrance into Helheim is that way. You should be safe by any means of travel." She studies the five dragons and Sleipnir again. "It would be near impossible for you to find your way to Niflheim from that path."

Eir's politeness puts us to shame. "Thank you."

The dimple shows on Hel's fleshy side as she smiles without much sincerity. "Good luck!"

Slowly, we depart, taking the stairs and careful not to damage any of the abundant gifts lining the way. As I climb onto Elan's back, a sense of relief washes over me even though we haven't completed or even started our task. Brushing up against Elan always brings me peace—that and the knowledge that we are leaving this realm. We fly over the bridge that leads to Hel's throne and keep an eye on Thor and Sleipnir. Silence rides with us, our minds filled with slashed hopes of bringing Balder home and the enormous task we face.

Slumping forward, I embrace Elan's neck as far as I can reach. "Do you think Thor has an idea how great this task is?"

Nope. I don't think he does. If you manage to achieve

this, then your group has completed the unthinkable. Her wings flap a few times, beating a soothing melody. *He should have bargained for a different deal.*

I expel a long breath. "I don't think he had much of a choice. It didn't look like Hel was ready to do much bargaining. It doesn't help that she likes Balder and wants his company."

Sitting up, I slide my hand under Elan's scale and connect with her dragon sight, searching for Thor in the darkness below. Sleipnir and Thor continue along the path, occasionally following instructions given by Elan.

Drogon, Tanda, and Naga, with their riders, scout ahead, keeping an eye out for Yggdrasil's entrance. They haven't wavered from the path that Hel has shown us, and it doesn't take long to reach the edge of the inlet, guarded as promised by Garm. Out of respect and not wanting to cause any more trouble, the dragons land.

The moment I climb off Elan, a piece of Helcake appears in my hand. I blink at it, disbelieving. Our motion to land and give the hound his due respect must have proved our hearts as pure.

A trail of drool falls from Garm's mouth, and his tail wags. "Oh, shucks! Are they for me?"

I hold out my piece. "It's certainly not for me."

Garm snatches it up without hesitation. "Usually,

I don't get a piece when people want to leave," he says with his mouth full. He swallows and eyes a piece that Elan holds in her talons. "To be honest, I don't usually get any souls that leave, so this is a nice treat." His red eyes glowing as if in excitement, he accepts a piece from everyone, all signs of aggression gone. Once finished, he stands to the side and waves us through the passage with a paw. "Of course you can leave."

Large rocks scatter the bank caked with mud and lead directly to the river Gjoll.

Instantly, my blood chills. Unpleasant memories of our last encounter with Modgud force their way into my thoughts.

The sound of swords whistling through the air does nothing to calm my nerves, Elan says.

"I can't hear the swords, but just seeing this river sends chills down my spine," I agree.

We approach the edge of the river, peer over the edge, and watch the swords traveling tip first in the water. A swirl of hands catches my eyes, and I turn in time to see Hildr waving her arms wildly as though conjuring a giant ball of magic.

"What are you—"

My words are cut short when she flings her cupped hands at the water, shooting it upstream. The water explodes, sending a shower everywhere. Water arches, and swords follow point first, accompanied by shards of ice.

"Damn it!" Hildr stomps her foot. "That was supposed to freeze the entire block. I was hoping that we could walk on this side of a frozen barrier that stopped the swords."

"Do you mean like we did with the water back on Midgard when Thor was trying to capture Jormungundr?" Britta asks.

"Yes. That's it!" Hildr exclaims.

Britta waves her hands, a motion that gathers a lot of magic. "Then why don't we try to make the wall, as we did in Midgard, together?"

Eir stands by her, and I join them, gathering magic. It hums in my fingertips.

"Ready?" Britta asks.

"Yes," we say in unison.

"Go!" Britta yells.

At once, we push our magic forward, watching the water rise, the top wanting to curve over our magic like a giant wave.

"We're going to have to make it bigger," Britta calls, spreading her hands apart, pushing one up and one down.

The wall of water increases, building higher, forming a wall as the swords point their angry tips and grow in numbers.

I clench my teeth from the effort, my body already screaming with exhaustion. My thoughts are conflicted. I want to cross the river without seeing Modgud again, yet at the same time, I want the pieces of Elan's soul and my soul back. I keep getting exhausted too quickly after having that piece taken from me.

The wall builds, and several more swords point downstream, their tips ominously indicating the spot we would walk through. We build the wall higher and manage to get it low enough to see the mud on the bottom. A thin path forms on the riverbed, broken by large puddles.

"We should be good to cross." Britta's voice is rough, almost a grunt.

Her face distorts with the strain of holding the magic. I study Hildr's expression then Eir's. They all look how I feel. I know I'm about to collapse. I hope that they are stronger than I feel.

Eir wipes her forehead on her sleeve. "We'll have to be quick if we're going to do this."

Without hesitation, Britta walks up to the edge first. "You lot follow me so we can hold this together. Thor and you dragons, get ready to walk on the far side of us."

"Done!" Thor answers for them all, grabbing Sleipnir's reins.

Britta places a foot onto the temporarily exposed riverbed. Suddenly, as though forced from behind, the swords pierce the wall of water and fly, following the course they should be traveling, cutting through the air.

Chapter Twenty-Four

With her talons, Tanda yanks Britta's uniform, dragging her onto the bank and sheltering her against her red scaly chest.

Shocked by the sudden onslaught of swords, we drop our barrier, releasing the water to flow its natural course.

Tanda pulls Britta away from the water's edge, holds her in front, and spins her around, studying her for any cuts or impalements. *Are you okay?*

Britta hangs limply in her grasp. "I'm fine. Thanks to you." Her shoulders slump farther as she catches sight of the river. "There goes all our effort. I don't think I could drum up enough energy to do it again."

Hildr shakes her head. "Me either. This water is more stubborn than the water on Midgard. It probably has some kind of magic buffer. It was fighting us the whole time."

Eir nods. "I felt it too."

I rub my arms, attempting to wipe away some of the strain. "I thought it was just me."

Hildr shakes her head. "It wasn't."

A somber mood cloaks the group as we watch the river flow past. We know we must wait for Modgud and her floating bridge. This time, I hope she will let us pass without claiming a part of someone's soul and honor her agreement with Elan and me.

After a while, Hildr regains enough energy to pace the bank, clenching her fists by her side. "I want to fight this nasty giant." She spins and walks in the other direction. "I want to fight her and teach her a lesson after what she did to you two." She stomps her foot. "But I'm also afraid that if I do anything aggressive, it may make the situation worse." She yanks at her short hair. "Argh!"

Eir stands by her and places a hand on Hildr's arm. "I don't believe fighting is the answer. It only seemed to make matters worse last time."

Hildr's chest caves. "I know. It's just so frustrating. I feel so useless. After what happened to Kara and Elan after our last effort..." She clenches her fist and waves it in front of her. "She better give back your souls, or else I might not be able to control myself."

I slide my hand around Elan's front leg and lean

against it. "We'll deal with it one step at a time. She promised to give the pieces of our souls back when we left if you didn't cause any trouble on Helheim. You did as promised."

Hildr's arms flop by her side helplessly. "But it's like making a deal with a murderer."

I rest my head against Elan's leg. "I know. But we can only take it as we get it. Don't stress before we have to tackle the situation. It will only make you more agitated. We could still be here for another half a day, waiting for the bridge to come by."

Thor pats down Sleipnir, and the horse whinnies. "We should be able to get every being to shed a tear for Balder, surely." A deep frown sets on his face, as though realizing what he's agreed to.

I straighten. "I'm not sure, Thor."

Finally released from Tanda's embrace, Britta stretches her arms. "It is quite a task. I, for one, will certainly do everything I can to make everyone shed a tear for Balder."

Hildr punches her fist against her palm. "Even if we have to make them cry."

"Hildr!" Eir cries. "I'm pretty sure that's not the way she wanted it to be done. She can probably tell if the tear was genuine grief or from a threat. I think that one will backfire."

Elan stiffens next to me. *There's been a change in the flight of the swords. I can hear it.*

A glint of gold catches my eye, and I turn to see the bridge drifting our way.

Britta watches the bridge's progression, her fingers picking at the hem of her uniform top. "Does this river crossing take us out of Helheim and to the right entrance into Yggdrasil to take us home?"

Thor's hand tightens around Sleipnir's reins, his eyes trained on the giantess. "I believe it does."

"Unless you manage to make a wrong turn in the world tree and end up on Niflheim." Hildr eyeballs Thor.

Thor chuckles and rubs the back of his neck. "Yeah, sorry about that. My mistake."

The bridge edges closer. The skeletal frame of the giant gatekeeper stands in the middle, her staff in hand and eyes fixed on us as though assessing us and weighing what she's going to do.

The rapid beating of my heart brings beads of sweat to my forehead. In an attempt to calm it, I place a hand over my heart, shushing it.

Elan nudges me with her leg. *You look exactly how I feel. Like you, I want the part of my soul back. We both deserve it. I just hope we don't have to fight for it. Any aggression sent her way last time didn't go too well.*

"I know what you mean," I say.

The bridge swinging from one hair stops in front of us, and Modgud walks to the end, peering down her nose at us. "Hmm. It seems that Hel was lenient on you. For what reason, I do not know."

Thor stares up at the giantess, his mouth agape. Eir slips slightly in front of him when he fails to speak, ignoring the giantess's dissatisfied comment. "Modgud. How lovely to see you again." She smiles sweetly. "We come in amity and wish to cross the bridge peacefully."

The silence is almost deafening as the guardian stares over us.

Eir continues, "We also hope and pray that you will return the pieces of my friends' souls." She indicates Hildr and Drogon. "My other friends respected your wishes and haven't caused any mischief in Helheim. You may ask Hel yourself if you like."

Dark, sunken eyes land on Hildr and Drogon then slowly travel over Elan and me.

"Is that so?" Modgud sounds unconvinced. "I find it hard to believe that Hel has let you leave unscathed."

Chapter Twenty-Five

We are bathed in silence as the gatekeeper processes her disappointment that Hel has left us in one piece. Each moment the silence continues, it becomes harder to breathe. Panic squashes my lungs, and the gatekeeper's superior response isn't helping, although something deep inside tells me it's only been a few moments.

The sunken eyes seem to focus on Eir. "You may go." She taps her staff then taps again, pushing Eir to the other side of the bridge without the Valkyrie having to take a step. A shocked cry reaches across the water from the other side of the bridge when the giantess does the same to Naga. The blue dragon lands behind his rider, accidentally nudging her off the bridge.

She then passes Sleipnir, then Thor, followed by Britta and Tanda. Slowly, Modgud lands her scrutinizing gaze on Hildr, and her eyes narrow at the fiery Valkyrie. "Have you truly behaved on this realm?"

Hildr straightens her shoulders yet tucks her chin. "Yes, I promise." Her voice is milder than usual. "And so has my dragon."

The sunken eyes land on Drogon, and he nods. *What she says is true.* He stands firmly on all fours and holds his head high. *We have kept our side of the agreement. Please give the sections of soul back to our friends.*

"I will do as I please." Modgud taps her staff, and both Drogon and Hildr project to the other side of the bridge, barely managing to stand when their feet hit the ground. I slip my hand under Elan's scale and catch the look of sadness on Hildr's face as she peers at us. She pulls at her earrings, a frown creasing her forehead.

When Modgud's eyes land on me, I cringe and worry my lip as she studies Elan. "Do you think you are deserving?"

Elan straightens, and I wish for some of her strength. *Yes. We do.*

"I was not talking to you, dragon," Modgud snaps.

I can feel the tension radiating off Elan as she holds back her retort. This time, the role of leader weighs strongly against her actions, and she knows which battle is worth fighting. A sense of eeriness passes over us as the gatekeeper's eyes scrutinize our every detail.

The echo of a tap startles me, and before I can register the meaning, I'm standing next to the skeletal giant. Her bony fingers dive into her fraying pocket and close around something before drawing it out. "From what I've seen, you have done as promised." She thrusts her palm over my heart, knocking me back a few feet. I stumble, trying to keep my balance as something warm enters my chest, bringing a strange sort of vitality. I welcome the strength that grows inside, and I smile. My body is overcome with tingles as though mending a rift. Before I can say anything, Modgud taps her staff on the bridge, and I'm shifted to the other side.

By the time I manage to turn, Elan is standing next to the giantess. I cross my fingers and grit my teeth, hoping for the best outcome for my magnificent friend. Modgud circles in front of her for quite some time, and I wonder if she thrives on making individuals stress. It certainly seems like it. Suddenly, her hand thrusts into her pocket before slapping against Elan's chest. Even Elan's enormous form stumbles backward from the force of the blow, yet her demeanor is relaxed and happy. She must have received her piece of soul back also. Modgud taps her staff, and in the blink of an eye, Elan lands at our end of the bridge.

"Well?" I call up to her.

"I got it back too." Elan jumps off the bridge and jigs.

A small cheer erupts through our friends as the bridge starts to pull away. Hopefully, we never have to deal with this ornery gatekeeper again. We huddle into a group at the start of the path that leads to the world tree. All eyes turn to Thor.

"Where do we start?" I ask.

The god runs a hand through his auburn hair, his fingers getting caught in the matted mess. "As far as I understand, we have two problems. Loki has escaped—"

Hildr raises a finger. "I believe Loki is still in his cell most of the time. He just occasionally shape-shifts and escapes temporarily."

"That's what I believe also," Britta says.

"I think he will cause mischief when he wants to. The typical Loki style, but for some reason, he still hangs around, pretending to be caught and fooling the majority," Hildr says.

Britta nods. "I vote we concentrate completely on getting Balder back to Asgard. We could certainly do with the likes of him and his beautiful face on our realm. There's no one else worth looking at."

Thor rolls his eyes. "Of course she has to say that." He folds his arms across his chest and stands with his legs splayed, a deep frown creasing his forehead. "We need to do this as quickly as possible. I know for sure that the Midgard serpent is still thrashing in the waters and causing trouble. The threat of Ragnarök remains close, and we don't have much time."

"What do you propose we do?" Eir asks.

Thor scratches his beard. "I propose we split up, each of us covering different realms. I will cover these lower realms. There aren't many living beings on Niflheim and Helheim. And after Kara's experience on Muspelheim, I can't send her there. It's best if I go."

"Can I take Alfheim?" Eir asks, her hands fidgeting nervously.

"Of course. You and Naga can go to the land of the elves. Hildr and Drogon should be a good fit for Midgard. I'll send a group to Svartalfheim and another to Jotunheim. It won't take long to do Asgard, as most there should have already shed a tear. That leaves Vanaheim. Kara and Britta, I think this will be a perfect spot for you two along with Elan and Tanda." Thor rubs his hands together, his eyes beaming with a mixture of apprehension and anticipation. "Let's go!"

. . .

THE END

ASSIGNED: book 7 in Thor's Dragon Rider series can be found on Amazon.

IF YOU ENJOYED SHROUDED, please take a few minutes and leave a review on Amazon. Thank you. Reviews help authors.

Get updates & notifications of giveaways

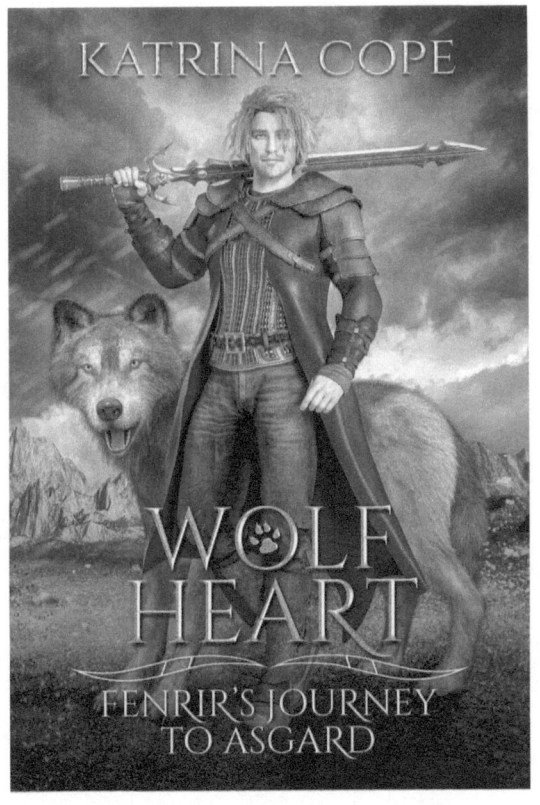

Would you like a FREE ebook?

Click here to get started: FREE copy of Wolf Heart: Fenrir's Journey to Asgard or go to https://BookHip.com/KQGGZF

Through this link you can sign up for my newsletter and

receive a FREE copy of Wolf Heart plus updates about my fantasy books, sales and notification of giveaways.

ACKNOWLEDGMENTS

Thank you to all of the creators of literature and websites who have spent time writing about Norse Mythology. Even though at times there has been contradicting information, it has been an interesting study. After all, of course a goat produces mead, and a dragon gnaws at the roots of the Yggdrasil, unhindered, threatening the existence of the nine realms attached to the world tree. Plus, there are many other "believable" tales told.

Norse mythology is such an impressive set of tales that I have incorporated some and invented others to create Kara and Elan's story.

I am touched by the enormous amount of support I have received from my immediate family. My husband has been a helpful first reader and, at times, been an excellent motivator, with hints of ideas to help me through the blanks. The support from my three sons has also been overwhelming. They have spent years putting up with my head in the clouds, thinking about the next plot twist or story, along with many hours spent working on my books and keeping in touch with my readers.

A big thank you to my extended family, who support me being a book enthusiast.

A huge thank you to my editor, Angela M., her editing and writing tips, and my proofreader, Alyssa B., for picking up the things we missed.

Thank you to all of my readers who have loved my work, and continue to read my stories.

BOOKS BY KATRINA COPE

Pre-Teen Books

The Sanctum Series

JAYDEN'S CYBERMOUNTAIN

SCARLET'S ESCAPE

TAYLOR'S PLIGHT

ERIC & THE BLACK AXES

ADRIANNA'S SURGE

~~~~~

Young Adult Urban Fantasy

Afterlife Series

FLEDGLING

THE TAKING

ANGELIC RETRIBUTION

DIVIDED PATHS

TRUTH HUNTER

Afterlife Novelette

THE GATEKEEPER

~~~~~

Young Adult Urban Paranormal Fantasy

Supernatural Evolvement Series

(Associated with the Afterlife Series)

WITCH'S LEGACY (Prequel)

AALIYAH

~~~~~

Young Adult Norse Mythology Fantasy

Valkyrie Academy Dragon Alliance

MARKED (Prequel)

CHOSEN

VANISHED

SCORNED

INFLICTED

EMPOWERED

AMBUSHED

WARNED

ABDUCTED

BESIEGED

DECEIVED

Thor's Dragon Rider

SAFEGUARD

PURSUIT

ENTRAPMENT

HOODWINKED

RELINQUISHED

SHROUDED

ASSIGNED

More to come

ABOUT THE AUTHOR

Katrina is a best-selling author of young adult fantasy and middle grade/tween novels. Her novels incorporate action, heart and an intriguing plot.

She resides in Queensland, Australia. Her three teenage boys and husband for over twenty years treat her like a princess. Unfortunately though, this princess still has to do domestic chores.

From a very young age, she has been a very creative person and has spent many years travelling the world and observing many different personalities and cultures. Her favourite personalities have been the strange ones, yet the ones under the radar also hold a place in her heart.

Katrina's online home is at www. katrinacopebooks.com

You can connect with Katrina on:

Facebook Group

facebook.com/Author.Katrina.Cope

twitter.com/Katrina_R_Cope

instagram.com/katrina_cope_author

pinterest.com/katrinacope56

bookbub.com/profile/katrina-cope

www.ingramcontent.com/pod-product-compliance
Lightning Source LLC
Chambersburg PA
CBHW020008140726
47904CB00018B/2119